"WILL YOU [illegible] mary shouted [illegible] whisper.

"Which way is that?" Gary whispered back at her. There was so much intimacy in his soft, hushed voice. And they had to stand so close to hear each other.

"Like you're in love with me. Like you can't keep your hands off me. Like we've even touched in the first place. Those people out there will have us sleeping together before the night is over!"

"Great, I'll take all the help I can get."

"This isn't funny, Gary," she hissed. "I have to live in this town, and I've already had to live down more than one scandal. I don't want to have to deal with another."

"If those people want to think that I'm in love with you and want to touch you, let 'em. There's nothing wrong with it. People do it all the time."

"I don't. Besides, it isn't true," she said softly.

"What if it *is* true? What if I fell in love with you the first time I saw you? What if I want to touch you so bad I ache . . . ?"

WHAT ARE *LOVESWEPT* ROMANCES?

They are stories of true romance and touching emotion. We believe those two very important ingredients are constants in our highly sensual and very believable stories in the LOVESWEPT *line. Our goal is to give you, the reader, stories of consistently high quality that may sometimes make you laugh, sometimes make you cry, but are always fresh and creative and contain many delightful surprises within their pages.*

Most romance fans read an enormous number of books. Those they truly love, they keep. Others may be traded with friends and soon forgotten. We hope that each LOVESWEPT *romance will be a treasure—a "keeper." We will always try to publish*

LOVE STORIES YOU'LL NEVER FORGET
BY AUTHORS YOU'LL ALWAYS REMEMBER

The Editors

TALK OF THE TOWN

MARY KAY McCOMAS

BANTAM BOOKS
NEW YORK · TORONTO · LONDON · SYDNEY · AUCKLAND

This "trashy romance" is dedicated
to my pals Nora and Pat
because you're both so . . .
full of it!
Romance, that is.

TALK OF THE TOWN
A Bantam Book / May 1995

LOVESWEPT and the wave design are registered trademarks of Bantam Books, a division of Bantam Doubleday Dell Publishing Group, Inc. Registered in U.S. Patent and Trademark Office and elsewhere.

ISBN 0-553-44486-7

Published simultaneously in the United States and Canada

Bantam Books are published by Bantam Books, a division of Bantam Doubleday Dell Publishing Group, Inc. Its trademark, consisting of the words "Bantam Books" and the portrayal of a rooster, is Registered in U.S. Patent and Trademark Office and in other countries. Marca Registrada. Bantam Books, 1540 Broadway, New York, New York 10036.

PRINTED IN THE UNITED STATES OF AMERICA

OPM 0 9 8 7 6 5 4 3 2 1

ONE

Her mother had always wanted her to go to college. Her father had never cared where she went. Grampa Earl simply mentioned that she was only going to get one shot at life, and she'd better make it a good one.

She was trying.

Her one good shot was streaking by—and it was wide of the target. Yet each morning she awoke with the realization that her life wasn't over. There was time for a gust of good luck to blow her back on track, for her shot to ricochet off a miracle and find a truer course. She was sure that stranger things had happened. To somebody. Somewhere. Trouble was, nothing strange ever happened to her.

It was a plain old Tuesday, her day off from her job at the diner. Trash day. Nothing too strange about that, except that trash day for Rosemary Wickum had nothing to do with setting her cans at the curb.

2

The secret to a successful trash day was to get there early.

She'd never been to a sale at Macy's or Lord & Taylor. In truth, she wasn't much of a shopper. When she had to shop, she was more of an impulse buyer than a be-practical-and-wait-for-it-to-go-on-sale bargain hunter.

Be that as it may, she could identify with the frenzied madness of the customers to get into the store, see everything, and buy, buy, buy before all the good merchandise was picked over and taken.

Dressed to browse in metal-toed boots, thick canvas overalls, and two sweatshirts to protect herself from sharp metal objects, she was quick to make decisions and accustomed to working for what she wanted. Certainly it was always wiser to be overdressed on these occasions, but she was already feeling uncomfortably warm and suspected that she'd be a wilting Rose Wickum before noon—another excellent reason to go early and get done as soon as possible.

The guard at the gate knew her truck on sight. No great feat, as once seen, her old green and gray pickup truck made a lasting impression on almost everyone. It had been patched more often than Raggedy Ann's bloomers and sounded remarkably like a Sherman tank. Still, it got the job done, and there was the added benefit of being waved straight through the gates without having to stop.

She was a bit surprised this time, though, when she waved to the guard in her usual fashion and received his detaining hand in response.

Talk of the Town

3

"Mornin', Rosie, how's it goin'?" he asked, stepping out of the glass-enclosed box of a guardhouse and into the shade of a huge sign that read All Bright Garbage—Recycling and Refuse Center.

"Good, Cletus. How about you?"

"I'm lookin' forward to a little excitement out here today."

"You are?" She frowned. "Did San Francisco deliver early?"

"No, no, same schedule. Somethin' new is in the works, and the boss is expectin' some grumblin'. He's hidin' out up here till it blows over."

Unlike the two of them, most people resisted living anywhere near a refuse center of any kind, refuse being what it is. A lot of garbage. Consequently, a really good garbage dump was hard to find. The residue of San Francisco's populace was transported by trailer trucks north along the rugged, lonely coastline to a landfill fifty miles east of Eureka. To a few people, such as Cletus and herself, San Francisco's bulky waste was generally considered to be some of the best within five hundred miles.

"Grumbling? What sort of grumbling?" she asked. "He's not closing this dump down, is he?"

He shook his head at her. "I've told you a million times not to call this a dump. We don't have dumps anymore. You can call it a recycling center or a refuse redistribution center, but not a dump."

"Do garbage trucks come in here and dump garbage?" she asked, teasing him.

"Every day." His smile showed big crooked teeth

and was exceedingly good-natured. "But we don't call them garbage trucks anymore. We call them recycling units when they come here and sanitation vehicles if they're heading for the landfill."

"Cletus, you're getting way too sophisticated for me," she said, smiling at him, squinting against the early morning sun. She tried to be as ecologically correct as the next person, sorting aluminum from glass and plastics, and saving what few newspapers came her way. But she was wholly disinterested in the technical mumbo jumbo of waste disposal and the new politically precise terminology that went with it. Garbage was garbage. "All I want is some interesting trash."

"And you're welcome to all you can carry out. I just thought you ought to know there might be some trouble out here today. The boss said people with picket signs, some screaming and yelling." He shrugged. "Nothin' serious, but you might not want to get caught up in it."

"What are they mad about now?"

"The boss announced last night that he's planning to build one of those big incinerators down in one of those little towns between Frisco and the capital, close to a new housing development. It was in the paper this morning. He said there was such a stink about it at the planning commissioner's office that he wanted to bus them all up to the landfill to see how they liked *that* stink."

"Well, I don't have anything to do with any of that. Why would they bother me?"

"I don't know that they would. I'm just warnin' you."

"Thanks. But I'll be fine."

"Okay. Let me know if you need any help."

"I will. See you later," she said, taking her foot off the brake and easing the old Ford into first gear.

For the record, combing through other people's discards wasn't exactly Rose's idea of a fun time. Rather, it was a necessary evil she performed with love and diligence in the name of self-expression. And All Bright's wasn't so bad. By definition it was dirty and smelly, but it was better organized than the local K Mart, in her opinion, well thought out and very tidy for a garbage dump. She would have readily admitted to preferring to do her junking there than in the old city dumps she remembered from her childhood—had anyone ever bothered to ask her.

She drove beyond a large building labeled MRF but pronounced "Murf," an abbreviation for *materials recycling facility*—garbage lingo has a way of rubbing off on you, you know. She passed the paper shed, which was hardly a shed but another large structure with tons of newspaper visible through the gaping entrance. Proceeding by a two-acre lot of pathetic looking automobiles waiting to be crushed and hauled away, she parked close to a similar-sized lot of *white goods.*

She wasn't sure why the mountain of scrap metal was called white goods except that it might have had something to do with the number of bathtubs, toilets, and refrigerators in the heap—mostly white, but it didn't really matter. It was an emporium of metal scraps, from fine wire to copper tubing; bread boxes to sled blades; television sets to baby strollers. And she was the first one there.

In an hour there would be twenty, maybe thirty more junkers scrambling over the hills and peaks of debris looking for salvageables. Most of her fellow scavengers would refurbish what they found that day and use it in their homes or sell it at a garage sale or a flea market.

Rose, however, would be putting her discriminate odds and ends to a higher, more aesthetic purpose and handled each one as if it were indeed a treasure.

Armed with a crowbar, wrench, pliers, and a few other small handy tools, she made several trips up and down the mound to place her carefully chosen pieces in the back of her truck—knowing from experience not to put anything down once recovered. Someone else would get it, or, more often than not, it would camouflage itself in the pile, disappear, and never be seen again. Garbage was garbage, after all, and eventually it all started to look the same.

Rose was average height—a minor disappointment to someone whose technicolor dreams had always revealed her ideal self as being gracefully tall and slender. Instead of willowy, however, she'd turned out several inches short of tall, slim, and amazingly strong. According to Grampa Earl, at least, her strength was amazing. She had a feeling that her physical strength was as ordinary as the rest of her body and that pumping her up was his way of getting out of helping her drag heavy metal objects home from the All Bright dump, but that was okay too. She liked to think she was amazingly strong. Amazingly anything, really.

Of course, she was no Atlas. She couldn't lift the world, and all too frequently her heart would claim a lovely piece of rubbish that her muscles couldn't budge.

Normally she would mark these precious parts with red plastic tape, fetch Cletus, another scavenger, or one of the yard workers, and together they would unwedge, uncover, untangle, and lift it free of its hopeless hiding place.

She picked up a training bike and tossed it several feet away, her eyes locked on a black wrought-iron candlestick. It was eighteen or twenty inches long, twisted but not bent. Stuck between the back of a clothes dryer and a lawn mower, it was tangled with something else she couldn't see.

She rammed the dryer several times with her hip, rocking it, but was unable to tip it over to get to the candlestick.

"Hey! Lady. You up there."

She turned her head to look down at a tall man standing near her truck. He looked like a fellow junk hunter in boots, grubby jeans, and a flannel shirt, with a five o'clock shadow before nine A.M. She was delighted to see him—and his muscles when he fisted his hands at his hips.

"Is all this stuff yours?" he asked, motioning to the huge pile of white goods beneath her.

"What?"

"Did you make this mess?"

"What?"

"You're going to have to pick it all up," he said with some authority. "You can't just dump stuff wherever you feel like it."

Rats. Clearly the man was delusional. Poor fellow. She went back to ramming the dryer.

"You don't have much of a sense of humor, do you?" he asked, taking the heap with a single bound, strutting toward her as if he were walking on a smooth, flat surface. "Or is it too early in the morning for junk jokes?"

He was grinning when he stopped before her. Grinning, and allowing his lively hazel gaze to dance across her face and hair and shoulders and lips and upper torso and . . . well, everywhere. He was so open with his admiration that she retreated a step, backed into the dryer, and landed smack on her fanny with a jolt of surprise.

He chuckled and motioned to the dryer. "Need a hand with that?"

She stared at him. There was still the possibility that the man was chemically controlled, but she was beginning to reconsider it. His eyes were too clear, his expression too animated for him to be on anything but a natural high.

"I need to roll it," she said dumbly. As an artist, she automatically noticed shapes and sizes in relationship to space and light. The man had broad thick shoulders that blocked the sun from her eyes.

"Okay. I'll help you."

She stood cautiously, watching him, all systems on standby.

"I've seen you out here before," he said, bending

over the bottom of the dryer while she positioned herself at its side. His big strong hands were dirty and stained with grease, she observed. "Two, sometimes three times a month. Always early in the morning."

Truth to tell, he watched for her. And since her visits were as irregular as his, he watched for her every time he was there. The thing was, she had a great gorgeous bush of red hair that would sparkle in the morning sunshine as if it were spun with gold. How could any man *not* notice something like that? And now that he was close enough to see that her almond-shaped eyes shimmered darkly green and mysterious like emeralds . . . well, she was very likely the prettiest woman he'd seen in twenty years—certainly since Cynthia McKissack in tenth grade.

She realized that she could have stepped away and let the man move the dryer alone, but she didn't. She had an overwhelming urge to appear ladylike, but it was hard to look urbane at a dump. It was her practice to act like an amiable but not too friendly, self-sufficient, overgrown tomboy—which was closer to her true identity anyway, she supposed.

"Do you work here?" she asked, pushing as he pulled on the big clumsy machine until it fell easily onto its other side and exposed the candlestick. She couldn't remember seeing him around the yard before—and she would have. You didn't see a smile, or a tush, like his every day.

"I own here," he said casually.

They straightened and looked at each other. One making passive assumptions, mildly surprised that a garbage man would be so . . . cute in an undefinable way. The other waiting to respond to whatever her reaction might be.

"So, you're Mr. All Bright."

She was saying it right, but he knew she had it spelled wrong.

"Gary Albright, All Bright Garbage, at your service."

She laughed. "Catchy. Very clever. You have great garbage here, Mr. Albright. This is my favorite dump," she said, thinking their conversation over, that they'd discussed all they could possibly have in common. "Thank you for your help."

She got down on her hands and knees to take a closer look at the candlestick. It had an electrical cord looped around the base several times; the appliance it was attached to was buried deeper in the drift somewhere.

"Actually this isn't garbage," he said, and he would have gone on to explain except that she put up a hand to stop him before reaching for her wire cutters.

"I know this one. I get this lesson every time I come. Garbage is table waste. Anything that isn't actual food waste is called trash or refuse," she recited, snipping at the cord. "I also know there aren't any more dumps. Dumps are landfills now, and this place is something entirely different."

"Very good," he said, sitting on the tipped dryer, stretching out his long legs as he watched her work. "You move to the head of the class."

"My friend Cletus is a very good teacher. Uses the

repetition method. Over and over," she droned, lifting the candlestick from its nest to admire it.

He chuckled. "Your friend Cletus, huh? Did your friend happen to mention that you might not want to be here today?"

"He certainly did," she said, getting to her feet. "He told me you were planning to entertain a few irate protesters for brunch this morning. I promise I won't get in your way."

"You can get in my way all you want. But the last time these folks came all the way up here to visit, they had recycling units backed up for ten miles in both directions, and regular traffic for another ten. You could be in my way for the next couple of days if you don't leave while you still can."

She grimaced at the thought. She imagined Lu detecting her absence at work the next day, notifying the police, then the media. . . . Rosemary Wickum Trapped in Stink at Garbage Dump. Not the kind of publicity she was looking for.

"You know, there's a lot that could be said for diplomacy and discretion," she said, deciding to take a rain check on the rest of the rubble and leave immediately. "It can get real inconvenient for people like me when people like you go around ticking people off with their bright ideas."

He stood and began to follow her down the mountain. "Wait'll you see how inconvenient it is when we're all knee-deep in solid waste."

"And what you're planning to do will prevent that?"

"What I'm planning is only a drop in the bucket.

Do you know that every man, woman, and child in this country alone produces three and a half pounds of waste every day? Altogether that's a billion pounds of rubbish a day, a hundred thousand seven-ton truckloads. Every single day."

"Messy business," she muttered, jumping off the rim of a bathtub to the ground.

"Right again," he said, landing beside her. He watched as she put the candlestick in the back of her had-it pickup truck, then stepped over to the driver's door.

"I have seventeen pieces here. Do I pay you or Cletus on my way out?" she asked, reaching inside the truck for her wallet.

She'd taken to his environmental passion like paper to a magnet.

"Cletus keeps track of it," he said, wishing he hadn't come at her so hard. He knew trash wasn't a tragedy for everyone. He felt it should be, but he knew it wasn't. "Look, I'm sorry I went off like that. I get carried away sometimes. I really can talk about other things. I actually went to college. I can speak on a variety of interesting topics."

"Is that right?" she said. Her look of amazement was quickly overcome by amusement—which worked out well. She appeared to be joking with him rather than disbelieving. But a college-educated garbageman? she'd thought, until she remembered the CPA she'd met working the day shift at McDonald's and an architect friend of hers who worked in a lumber mill to support his family. It was a sign of the times, and she felt bad for him.

"I have degrees and everything," he went on blithely. "I did my master's thesis on the history of trash."

"It has a history?"

"It is history," he said mildly, wishing he hadn't gotten back on that track so fast. "After they find the bones in the burial grounds, archaeologists head straight for the nearest land elevation to find out what the people were like. When they lived. How they lived. What they used to live. The homes and books and paintings of ancient civilizations are gone, but their trash is still there."

That was mildly interesting, but . . .

"You make it sound like something alive. With an ancient past and a horrible future. Like one of those old Japanese sci-fi movies with this thing living in the ground, growing bigger and bigger, getting ready to take over the earth and destroy the world."

"You know, that's not a bad analogy," he said, shaking his finger at her thoughtfully. "Do you have a piece of paper and something to write with? I want to get that down before I forget it."

"Are you serious?"

"Yes. I have to give a talk to the National Solid Waste Management Association in a couple of months. The thing could breathe methane gas and excrete leachate. It's great." He paused. "You don't mind if I use it, do you?"

"Knock yourself out." She couldn't quite believe

this guy was real . . . and sober. Or that there was a national association of garbagemen for that matter. But she crossed out the front of one of her bank deposit slips and handed it to him—she never used up all her deposit slips before she ran out of checks anyway. "That's the only paper I have; you can use the back. Here's a pen."

"Thanks," he said, taking them eagerly. He glanced briefly at the front of the slip, then used the rim of her truck bed as a desktop. "As much as I appreciate you letting me use your mind like this, that's not why I came over here."

"Of course not. How could you know I had it with me, right?"

He looked at her, then grinned. "Right." He hesitated briefly. "I came to see if you'd go to dinner or a movie with me sometime. Actually I came over to see if you were wearing a wedding ring. And I know that just because you're not wearing one, that doesn't mean you're not married or living with someone, but it's a good enough reason to at least ask and find out."

A doorknob could see his intentions. He was attracted to her. And she was flattered. Sort of. She liked him. He was certainly interesting in an unusual way, and he was definitely cuter than your average garbageman, but . . . he was a garbageman.

"I'm not married, but I'm not really dating right now either," she told him as kindly as she could. "It was nice of you to ask, though."

"Nothing nice about it," he said, looking disappointed but far from defeated. "I think I'd do just about anything to touch that red hair of yours."

Maybe it wasn't drugs. Maybe he was just plain crazy.

"If I'm going to go, I'd better . . . go," she said, opening the door of the truck as serenely as possible to hide the turmoil she was feeling. She wasn't sure if she should start screaming for help or giggle and bat her eyes at him. "It's been nice meeting you, um . . . ?"

"Gary."

"Gary."

"Would you mind giving me a lift to the front gate? It gets to be a long walk after a while."

"Sure. Get in."

"I'll just ride along here, if that's okay," he said, stepping onto the runner and clamping a big hand on the door frame. "Watch the potholes."

She shifted into neutral and turned the key. The old truck never started on the first go-round, or the second. But by the sixth try she had the sinking feeling something was wrong.

"Engine's flooded," he said, stepping down from the runner to stand in the window. "Give it a few minutes and try again."

"You wouldn't believe how many times I've thought about parking this old thing over there by the crusher and walking away," she said, acutely aware of being stared at. "But I always feel as if I'd be burying it alive somehow."

"It does have . . . personality." She laughed softly

and nodded. "What do you do with all the stuff you collect?" he asked.

"I elevate it to a higher station, give it a new purpose, a new importance," she said, as eloquent as she was facetious. "I transform it from mere stuff to objets d'art."

"No kidding. So you're an artist."

"Don't I look like I'm starving?"

"Not exactly. You look beautiful."

Oh, right. In steel-tipped boots and overalls. No makeup. She was tempted to lean over to the rearview mirror to check her hair, but it hardly mattered at this point. The man wasn't on drugs and he wasn't insane, he was simply full of garbage.

Nevertheless, a disconcerting warmth rose up her neck and burned in her cheeks under his conspicuous regard. She lowered her eyes and looked away, bent forward and tried to start the engine again.

"What's your name? Are you famous?"

"Not hardly. I've sold a couple pieces, but Rosemary Wickum isn't exactly a name you'll hear bounced around with Boccioni and Gabo for a while yet."

Sensitive as ever to any mention of the crusher, the old bucket of bolts decided to behave itself. The engine turned over without a sputter.

"Maybe that's good," he said, jumping back on the runner. "I've never heard of those guys anyway. So, maybe you'll be bigger than both of them."

She rolled her eyes. As if being a Master of Trash automatically made him an art critic.

"Would you like me to keep a lookout for interesting pieces and put them aside for you?" he bellowed into the window, raising his voice over the cacophony of the truck.

"Thanks, but I pick my pieces like New Age freaks pick out their rocks. If I'm in the right place at the right time and it calls out to me, then we were meant to be together. It's a very subjective thing."

"Like meeting people."

"That's right. What interests you might not interest me at all."

"Or we could have similar tastes and you'd be missing out on some really good pieces. You never know." She bobbed her head as if to admit that it was possible, but not likely. "We should definitely go out then, get to know each other better, compare tastes."

Kissing came to her mind. Comparing tastes with their mouths. A distracting thought. So much so, she forgot to drive around the next pothole.

"Awwwwwww."

The truck came to a standstill in a cloud of dust. She turned off the engine and left it shuddering as she leaped out.

"Are you all right?" she asked, running past the tailgate and falling to her knees beside his lifeless looking body. "Are you hurt? Can you hear me?"

He tried to nod his head and grimaced.

"I'm so sorry. I didn't even see it. Are you hurt?"

He rolled his head back and forth. He patted his chest and took in great gulping gasps of air.

"Are you all right? Talk to me."

"Just . . . winded." He tried to sit up.

"Stay still a minute. Good grief, I could have killed you. Why couldn't you ride inside with me? You should have. Are you all right? Are you hurt?"

"No. I'm okay. I just need to . . . catch my breath," he said haltingly. She was more worried than angry with him, and he liked that. The anger and the worry. It made her eyes an even darker green and her skin paler, more delicate looking.

"You scared me to death," she said, placing a hand over her quaking heart, a movement he didn't miss. But with the sweatshirts and overalls, his curiosity as to what lay beneath was simply more piqued.

"I'm sorry. I wasn't paying attention," he said, sitting up slowly. She sighed and sat back on her legs, her hands on her thighs. He looked up from her lap with a foolish smile. "I was worried you'd leave before I could convince you to go out with me."

She scowled at him. "I told you—"

"I know what you told me. I'd just . . . well, I'd like to see you in something other than those overalls once. And get to know you. It doesn't even have to be a date. We could meet for coffee or a drink somewhere. Before dark. In broad daylight. You could bring a big ugly friend to make sure I don't step out of line."

"But why?" she asked, thinking it a logical question. She was only average height, and very strong. Her hair was too curly. Her nose was too thin and turned up on the end and covered with freckles. Her right eyetooth was a little crooked. The only truly remarkable thing about her was that she created beauty in metal, and he hadn't seen any of her work.

"Why not? We both collect junk. We both recycle it. Who knows what else we might have in common?" She gave him a suspicious eye. "Truly. I like to eat, do you?"

In spite of her misgivings, she laughed.

"You're crazy. You know that, don't you?"

"Sure. I have to be. Look at what I do for a living."

"There's nothing wrong with what you do." Somebody had to do it, right?

"Fighting a losing battle is crazy," he said.

"You're not losing. Things are getting better. I read not long ago that the hole in the ozone was beginning to heal itself. You must be doing something right."

"Not fast enough. And dealing with other people's trash is as bad as being a mortician. Everybody needs us, but no one wants to dance with us. Besides me and Cletus, how many garbagemen do you know? Have you ever gone out and introduced yourself to the guys on the trucks? Have you ever even talked to one before?"

She tried to recall. Then shook her head.

"Do you speak to your mailman?" he asked, questioning in a natural, tolerant manner.

"When I see him."

"If you were in a room full of people, could you pick out the men who pick up your trash?"

"I don't think so," she said after a moment's consideration.

"What about your mailman?"

"Sure, he—" She stopped when she got his point.

"You see? We're like invisible people who haul away the used and unwanted. No one sees us. No one talks to us. No one says thank you. No one decorates their trash can at Christmastime the way they do their mailboxes. We do more for the health and preservation of the world than some doctors and lawyers I've heard of, but we're never invited to Career Day at school. Parents say, 'Study hard, son, or you'll end up being a garbageman for the rest of your life.' We're at the bottom of the barrel. Nobody loves us. Doesn't wanting to be one sound a little crazy to you?"

"Well, you went to college," she said. "You have degrees and can speak on a variety of subjects. Why'd you become a garbageman?"

"It's in my blood," he said, grinning as she teased him with his own words. He got to his feet, dusting the dirt from his dirty clothes. "My dad was a garbageman and both my brothers are in the refuse business."

"You're kidding," she said, amazed, amused, and appalled all at once. He looked at her as if to say "You see?"

"My younger brother has an operation similar to this one on the East Coast, and my older brother is up in the Northwest excavating old dumps and landfills."

"Ugh. What for?" she asked, taking his lead as he walked around the truck to get in.

He gave her an odd look, then went on to explain as he stepped up into the cab. "The old dumps and landfills are leaking leachate, that's, ah, well, it's rainwater usually, that falls on these places and it filters down through the waste. It carries germs and polluting chemicals with it, into the ground below and into the water table. Also," he said, opting not to mention that the truck's engine was flooded again as the expression on her face was already showing signs of annoyance, "recycling is relatively new, so he'll remove the glass and metals, line the bottom of the pit with plastic, clay, and gravel, and refill it with the decomposing waste."

"So, it's like a government cleanup program."

"Not really," he said, watching her rub the palms of her hands back and forth along the canvas of her overalls as if she were nervous or anxious for something to happen. "There's a little government funding, but it's a private enterprise. My brother will keep what he makes from the recycling and he'll pipe out the methane gas, which is a by-product of decomposition, and sell that to heat homes and the like. And in return for the government financing, he'll also pull out the leachate, purify it, and return it to the water system."

"So everyone wins."

"Pretty much."

"Who thinks up all this stuff? And why didn't they think of it sooner?" she said, wondering aloud as she tried the engine again. Heavens above, it would have saved a lot of time and panic if they had, she thought, neither expecting nor really wanting an answer to her questions. She'd forgotten for a moment who was sitting beside her.

"Who wants to think about trash when there are empires to be built and wars to be fought and trips to the moon to be made?" he asked, disappointed when the engine turned over. He could have sat there all day talking to her, looking at her. "It's like a disease. No one wants to think about it if it only affects a few people. But when it becomes an epidemic and you get it, or someone you love gets it, well, that's a whole new story. Every brilliant mind in the world goes to work on it. And once in a while the solutions are so simple, it's embarrassing."

"It is, isn't it? Embarrassing. Not just that some of the solutions are simple, but that we've let it get so far out of hand."

He nodded, silently accepting his share of the blame. The front gate was in sight. There were a few cars parked along the fence already, but not so many that he'd be afraid to send her through. Unfortunately.

Being a college-educated garbageman was making a little more sense to her. Trash wasn't what it used to be. It wasn't simply picked up and dumped anymore.

"I know they don't offer garbage degrees in college. What did you study?" she asked, curious.

"Science. I had a double major in biology and chemistry. I mastered in environmental science. Took a little law, too, for a while."

"But you're not a lawyer."

"No. I'm a garbageman." And proud of it, she could see. "You can let me out here."

She stopped near the MRF.

"Well, you've been a real education, Gary," she said, preparing to say good-bye to him, more than a little befuddled. Nothing he'd said made an impact on her life, really. It had been marginally interesting, and he was a likable man. But that was all. So why was she finding it hard to leave him? "Between you and Cletus,

I'm starting to feel like an informed citizen. Those must be the protesters there, huh?"

" 'Fraid so." He drummed his fingers on his knee, looking at the small crowd of people beyond the gate, some three hundred feet away. "Not much of a turnout this time."

"Do they make you nervous?" she asked, detecting a subtle change in his demeanor.

"They make me mad."

She might have asked why. She might have even questioned him about the incinerator project he was planning, to be polite. But he started to get out.

"When will you come back?" he asked, holding the door open.

She shrugged. "When I need more stuff to work with."

"You're not going to make this easy, are you, Rosemary?"

She could have pretended not to know what he was talking about, but it wasn't her way.

"I think making your acquaintance was very easy. And very nice. I hope to see you again sometime."

"Count on it."

She smiled and waved and thanked him for his help again as she drove away. She probably wouldn't brag to her friends that a garbageman had tried to pick her up at the dump, but his attentions had pleased her in a deeply feminine fashion. No woman ever got enough of that sort of consideration, did she?

TWO

She turned off the flame of the blowpipe and pushed back the mask on the welding hood to take a fresh look at her work. The metallic sculpture stood tall and graceful, but there was something wrong with it. Something as basic as breathing, but she couldn't put her finger on it.

She sighed, discontented, and shook her head. She could always ask Justin to come up and take a look at it, get his opinion. . . . No, she wasn't quite ready for that. In another week or two maybe, she decided, her shoulders drooping with fatigue. She turned off the acetylene gas by way of the valve at the top of the tank. She'd done all she could for one day.

She removed her thick gloves and the hood, picking up a soft towel she kept nearby to wipe the sweat from the back of her neck. She always worked with the fans blowing and the doors open, but even tying her hair back in a ponytail did little to ease the heat inside the hood.

But it wasn't the unseasonably hot spring weather or the heat from the torch or the physical exertion or the size of the hood that was steam-cooking her brain. She'd had her creative juices cranked up to high on a front burner for so long, they were boiling over, spilling down the sides of her inventive pot of thought, flowing uselessly, going to waste, turning to black carbon and more steam in a flame of futility.

Her last three works had fallen miles short of her expectations. She looked at them, grouped a few yards away, outside the ring of bright light she'd been working in. They were finished, but they weren't complete. Justin wouldn't let her work on them anymore. He said they were perfect. Beautiful. Magnificent. But they weren't.

They were big, clumsy, and awkward. They were like stepchildren she wanted to love, but she just couldn't seem to bond with them. Whatever they needed wasn't in her to give, and the hopes she might have had for them simply weren't there anymore.

She drank lukewarm water from a plastic bottle and turned her back on them as she screwed the top back on. The longer she looked, the harder she studied them, the further away the answer seemed. She was hungry. She wanted a bath. She needed to sleep.

The past few nights had been fitful and bothersome. She dreamt over and over of an elegant ball at the All

Bright dump. The King of Trash—who looked a lot like Gary the garbageman—was about to announce his choice of a bride, but he hadn't yet seen Rose. Her overalls were dirty and her son Harley's smelly high-tops were the only shoes she could find. She jumped up and down and waved frantically as he passed by on his bulldozer, but she couldn't catch his attention. If only he would look at her. See her. She pushed her way past hundreds of people with picket signs, her heart racing with desperation. If he didn't know she existed, he'd never know how much she loved him or what a wonderful life they could share. Then, just as she was about to pull the lever on the magic trash compactor that would turn all the King's trash into golden eggs and prove to the King and the kingdom, once and for all time, that she was worthy of being his Queen . . . she'd wake up in a cold sweat.

And so it was, with rose-scented bubbles clinging to her skin, her hair pinned high up on her head, her muscles just beginning to unravel, her mind pondering the insanity of the subconscious, that she heard a knock on the door downstairs.

The second time she heard it, she stopped stirring the bubbles with her finger and frowned, listening intently. She heard nothing.

"Someone's at the door," she hollered to be heard through the bathroom door. Still nothing. "Earl? Harley? Will you get the door?"

A third knock.

"Is anyone out there?" Silence. "Harley? Oh, for crying out loud," she muttered, reaching for a towel.

"I'm going to wring his neck," she said, speaking of her grandfather, who had a tendency not to hear much beyond the call to dinner unless he wanted to.

She pulled the door open with the towel wrapped around her, bubbles popping on her legs and ankles, water pooling at her feet, and was dumbfounded to find the room empty. She padded over to the stairwell and called, "Who's down there?"

"Gary Albright," came a muffled voice.

"Who?"

"All Bright Garbage. Gary. We met on Tuesday."

She waddled a wet route across the room to the window facing Beach Street and peered down. There in the twilight stood the King of Trash.

"Hi."

He stepped away from the door to look up at her. The lamplight at her back glowed warm and golden in her hair and along the naked slope of her shoulders. She looked like something out of a fairy tale. He felt something swelling inside, filling empty places he didn't know he had.

"Hi," he said, a slow and remarkably bright grin spreading across his face. "I was wishing you wouldn't be in overalls, but this is much more than I'd hoped for."

"What are you doing here?" she asked, sidestepping the window so all he could see was her head and neck. She hadn't fallen asleep in the tub, had she? She wasn't back in that crazy dream, was she? "How did you know where I lived?"

"From the deposit slip you gave me, remember?

Your address was on the front." A stupid and dangerous mistake she would never make again, she decided immediately. "I brought you some stuff," he said, indicating the box at his feet. "I know you said you like picking out your own, but I needed an excuse to come see you."

"What for?"

"For whatever you do with it. I was curious about that too. I'd like to see it."

"No. I mean, what did you need an excuse to come see me for?"

"Well, I didn't know how you'd take to me showing up on your doorstep, so I figured I'd bring along some reason for being here, in case I got bashful at the last minute." He grinned. Bashful wasn't really a problem for him. "This wasn't an easy place to find, you know. It's right where it's supposed to be, but I kept looking for a house or an apartment. I've never met anyone who lived in a gas station before."

"And now you have," she said, glancing across the not-so-busy main street at Lulu's, the diner where she spent the better part of her life cleaning and scrubbing and waiting on tables. The door had opened and her grandfather and teenage son were coming out. "Look. I don't mean to be rude or unfriendly, but . . ."

"But you're going to be anyway, because you hardly know me and you're not in the habit of inviting strange men into your home. I understand that. So, why don't you come out here, look at the stuff I brought, talk to me a little while, and get to know me better? Then the next time I come, I won't be so much of a stranger." He held his hands out in a pleading manner to tease her.

"You don't even have to change what you're wearing. Just come down as you are."

He was tickling the deeply feminine thing inside her again, and she smiled.

"Hey, Mom," Harley called, his changing voice deep and manly this time. His carrot orange hair was probably longer than it should be . . . and hardly ever combed. His arms and legs were long and skinny, gangly looking from growing so much over the winter. Going through what only a loving mother could refer to as a homely phase, he wore braces on his teeth and had a small rash of pimples on his chin. Still, looking at him was the only thing in the world that could bring a spontaneous smile to her lips. "Lu wants to know if you had time to clean the gunk out from under the fryer today."

"Run back in and tell her yes," she called to him, watching Grampa Earl walk in a distinctly lumberjack style as he crossed the road. She'd often wondered if the gait was hereditary—Harley having a similar posture—and if so, was ever grateful that it was recessive in her. It was a bold, manly stride, and she felt she was much too short and too female to do it justice.

"Earl, this is Gary Albright," she said when she noticed the old man eyeing her guest. "Gary, this is my grandfather, Earl Wickum. The boy is my son, Harley Wickum," she added, getting the family secret out and over with.

It didn't take long for most people to figure out that the three of them had the same last name, and what that meant about her and Harley. She rarely offered details, but she never tried to hide it. And most people were polite enough to let it go at that, no matter what they were thinking.

Gary, however, wasn't connecting any dots. By the time a man reached thirty, most of the available women he met either had children or were looking to have them—immediately. Eight or nine years later, dating single mothers was just part of the game.

"How do you do, sir," he said, holding a friendly hand out to Earl before he really noticed that the old man's were both full, a large styrofoam cup in each.

"Humph," Earl grunted with a nod of acknowledgment. He was as chatty as he was deaf—not at all.

"Here, let me get that door for you," Gary said, reaching out to turn the doorknob for him. "Those chocolate sundaes sure look good."

Earl walked past him and into the garage. Rose could hear him on the stairs before Gary looked back up to the window. Harley was leaving the diner again.

"Should I come up, or will you come down?" Gary asked, knowing an open door of opportunity when he saw one.

"You should go home," she said, not unkindly.

"But I brought stuff. Don't you want to come down and look at it?"

"Not really. I told you, it has to speak to me. When it speaks to someone else, it never works for me."

"It might be different this time. The three of us could be speaking the same language," he said, indicating the box as if it were a third person.

Harley had crossed the street and come up behind Gary. He was staring at the box, hoping there was a midget inside. This was no small man before him, and Harley didn't relish the idea of confronting him if he was hassling Rose. He spooned in another mouthful of hot fudge sundae, thinking it might be his last.

"You can leave the box if you want, but I've had a long day and I'll probably have another one tomorrow, so I—"

"Hey, Harley, how are you?" he said, cutting off her dismissal when he noticed the boy behind him. He put out his hand for a friendly shake—waiting patiently while Harley wiped his sticky fingers on his shirtfront before taking it. "I'm Gary Albright. I met your mom a few days ago, and she's making me crazy," he said, only half joking. "She won't even talk to me. I have a steady job. I've never been to jail. I don't smoke or lie or cheat on my taxes. I do have an occasional drink, usually a beer with the boys, but I haven't gotten sloppy drunk in years. I am divorced, but I don't have any children, and I own my own home in Fairfield. That's about halfway between San Francisco and Sacramento, which works out pretty well because I do a lot of business in both places . . . and it's pretty quiet out there, away from all the big city hubbub. My friends think I'm a pretty decent kind of guy, but I can't get your mother to give me the time of day. What should I do?"

Harley was still shaking his hand, nodding, his mouth hanging open in dumb disbelief. Over the years, other men had come sniffing around his mother. Only a few had paid him the slightest heed; most disappeared in light of her indifference; none of them had ever asked his advice.

He shrugged, his hand dropping to his side when Gary released it.

"Do you have a girlfriend?" Gary asked.

He shook his head.

"But there's a girl you like a lot, isn't there?"

Heather Underwood. Pale yellow hair. Big, bright blue eyes. Big breasts and long legs . . . Harley shrugged and moved his head a little. Gary saw it as a definite maybe.

"Then you know how it is," he said, demonstrating the male bond between them. "Getting a particularly fine lady to notice you're alive or to speak a few kind words to you can make you a little nuts sometimes. Women are hard to figure, unless there's someone around to help you out. What do you say? Got any pointers for me?"

Harley looked up at his mother. *His mother*, not a particularly fine lady in his opinion, but a pretty good mom nonetheless. He liked her, most of the time. There didn't seem to be any good reason why some other man wouldn't like her, too, he supposed. His stomach made a sudden queasy flip. Man, what if this Albright guy was thinking of his mother the way he thought about Heather?

"Where'd you find this one?" he asked her, all too aware of her amusement. That was always a good sign—something the man would want to know if he felt like telling him, which he didn't.

"At the dump," she said, half laughing.

"The dump?" He looked back at Gary, surprised. At fourteen, even he knew that the dump was no place to pick up babes—not that his mother was a babe in the first place.

Gary made a helpless gesture. "She stood out like a diamond in coal. A silk purse in a pile of sows' ears. A Rose in a weed garden. What could I do?"

Rose laughed aloud and her son frowned.

"You need help, mister."

"I know. That's what I've been trying to tell you."

Along with his homely phase, poor Harley was also going through a period of unpredictable mood swings. She often thought of him as a two-headed monster. One pure sweet Harley, the other a ghoul from the gates of hell. And she never knew which head she was talking to or which would react first. He still laughed sometimes, but he didn't take to teasing and joking as well as he used to. She could tell by his stance that he wasn't enjoying Gary's jovial disposition.

"Okay. You win," she said, hoping to defuse the situation. "I'll change and be down in a minute."

She put on jeans and a T-shirt in a hurry. Harley was a smart kid who knew not to pick a fight he couldn't win, and Gary wouldn't dare raise a hand to her son if he knew what was good for him. Still, he was a strange stranger, and she hadn't been able to describe Harley's behavior as anything but weird for the past twelve months. She didn't like leaving the two of them alone.

As was often the case, she was right to worry, but her concerns were once again misplaced.

"Most of these are collectibles," Harley was saying as she came barefooting through the door of what once had been the business office. They were hunkered down beside the box together, looking for all the world to be old pals. "Mom brings 'em home sometimes and gives 'em to Janice Tharp. She has the antique store a few blocks down, just before you get back on the highway. She fixes 'em up and sells 'em. I can't see it myself, but you wouldn't believe how many people collect these old lanterns. What's this?"

"I wasn't sure at first, but I think it's a waffle iron. It opens up here, see?"

"Stokin'," he said, turning the black disclike object over in his hands with interest. "She says it's part of the magic, you know? To get something as strong as steel to bend to her will, to get it to do what she wants it to do. Even steel beams in an unfinished building are a big deal to her." He put the waffle iron back in the box. "But she won't use any of this. Justin says it's distracting." He said the name as if it left a cod liver oil taste in his mouth. "He says it pulls the focus of the work to another time and place . . . whatever that means."

"It means that people spend more time trying to figure out what everything in the piece was used for, than in trying to see what the artist is trying to say through his work," she said, walking up to them.

Harley rolled his eyes and Gary stood to greet her.

"Hi," he said, his voice like a warm, intimate caress. The expression on his face was even less settling. His pleasure at seeing her was embarrassing—and nice, in a long-forgotten way.

"Hi," she said, feeling an urge to squirm. She looked down at the box, taking a quick inventory.

"Nice. But . . . you won't mind if I pass these on to Janice, will you?"

"No. You can put them back in the trash if you want. They've served their purpose here." All he wanted was to stand close to her again. "Who's Justin?"

"A friend," she said, hesitating. "An art dealer in San Francisco. He gives me advice and is acting as my agent for a while."

"Some agent," Harley muttered, getting to his feet. "Show him what he's making you do."

Making you do? The words twisted Gary's stomach and furrowed his brow.

"He's not *making* me do anything," she told them both, but spoke directly to Harley.

"He's not letting you do what you want to do. He's making you unhappy. You hate what you're doing."

"No, I don't," she insisted, needing to be convinced as much as Harley did. "He just suggested that I try something a little different, a little more commercial, to get started. That's all."

"Come'ere and look at this stuff," he said, slapping Gary on the sleeve with the back of his hand. He led the way to his mother's makeshift studio in the old garage.

"Harley, they're not ready," she said, following third in line. She was half angry, anxious, and feeling very defensive. "They're not done. I'm not ready to show them yet. Please. He's a garbageman. He doesn't know anything about art. . . . No offense."

"None taken." Gary was having a grand time. The kid was coming around. Rose was nervous. He was being included in a family dispute, and he was going to see her work. Things were working out just fine.

"You're really a garbageman?" Harley asked, turning abruptly. "You work at the dump?"

"Sometimes," he said, nodding.

"Nitro." He looked impressed.

When he continued into his mother's studio, Gary turned to her and said, "See? Kids, dogs, and flies love me. How bad can I be?"

She didn't mean to chuckle, but she did. And it took some of the edge off having him look at her sculptures. She stood in the doorway as he approached the newest piece, studied it, walked around it twice, and then moseyed over to the three standing off to the side. When he finally turned to face her, his expression made her heart sink deep in her chest.

"Your mom's right. I don't know anything about art. I wouldn't know where to begin to say whether this is . . ."

"You know junk when you see it, don't you?" Harley asked, unreasonably angry in Gary's estimation. That he had strong feelings about his mother's work was clear, but agreeing with him might not be wise either.

He glanced briefly at Rose before trying to answer. "Usually. But one man's junk is another man's—" He stopped when the boy held up both hands.

"Okay. You wanted my advice, so here it is."

"Harley . . ." she said in warning. The boy was out of control again. There was no doubt about it anymore, she was going to have to kill him one of these days.

"Don't lie to her. She flips out."

"She flips out?" The kids were always the best and most honest source of information on the mother—something else he'd learned early on in his dating career.

"Goes ballistic. She says I can rob banks, but I better not ever lie to her again. Come here. Look at these," he said, walking to the corner of the room behind the three iron sculptures to pull at a tarpaulin cover.

"You're really pushing it," she warned him a second time.

Under the tarp was a table covered with metal objects. Others sat on the floor below. The closer Gary got to them, the easier it was to see how different they were from the larger, bulkier sculptures he'd just looked at. These pieces were intricate. Where the others were fluid and graceful, these were distinct, defined . . . delicate almost.

Several pieces were a mixture of metal and stained glass. A little like church windows, but finer with multifarious metal work on each, so that every cut of glass was a work of art inside a work of art. There were copper and bronze pieces as well, elaborate and complex; multifaceted pieces that were a study of labor and intense thought and emotion.

Gary knew little of art, it was true, but he knew what he liked.

"These are incredible. Really beautiful," he said, his voice hardly more than a whisper that echoed through the old garage. Picking up one piece he was most intrigued with, he added, "It must have taken you hours and hours to do this."

"That's a good one," Harley said, approving his choice. "I like those two there too. She used to sit down here and work on these at night. She even sold two of them once. But Justin has her convinced there's no market for them. He's got her welding those jungle gyms together."

Okay. No more warnings. Three strikes. Harley was outta there.

"All right, Harley, that's enough," she said, finally moving away from the door. "You and I have had this conversation before, and Gary doesn't need to hear it. Go find something else to do. Now."

"Like what?"

"Homework?"

"Done it."

"TV."

"Seen it."

"Clean your room?"

"Been there. Don't want to."

"Then go out and chase cars, but *go now.*"

"This is good," he said as he walked by Gary. As stormy as his emotions had been moments earlier, he was just as calm and playful now. "She wants to be alone with ya, man. I'm warnin' ya though, treat her bad and I'll . . . me and Grampa'll be down on you like flies on—"

"Harley."

". . . at a picnic."

"See ya, Harley," Gary said, listening to the boy's slow, reluctant steps on the stairs between the office and the garage.

"Not if I see you first, man."

Rose sighed loud and long-suffering. "If he hadn't been such a cute, sweet little boy, I'd pay someone to drown him."

"Well, you couldn't very well do it yourself. He's a big boy."

She nodded. "It's unnatural. Kids shouldn't be allowed to get bigger or smarter than their parents until after they leave home."

"He's okay for a kid his age."

"Says the father of none," she said, picking up the tarpaulin and throwing it back over the table.

"Says an objective observer who's seen his share of really rotten kids," he said.

She detected a sharp edge to his voice and kept her back to him. She glanced down at the few uncovered pieces of metal sculpture on the table and felt a frustrated need to cry. She was tired; put out with and constantly worried about Harley; unhappy with her work, her life, and the rapid passage of time. She didn't know if Gary wanted a child, but if he ever had, her words had been cruel.

"You're right," she said, arranging the canvas over the table, carefully hiding what she loved to do so she could concentrate on what she felt she had to do to get her work noticed. "That was uncalled for and . . . well, you're right about Harley. He's not a bad kid. I get so wrapped up in him sometimes, I forget to stand back and take a good look at him." She turned to look at Gary then. He was still holding the stained glass design he favored in both hands. "Those with the glass are prettier in the light," she said, motioning him into the circle of brightness in the middle of the room. He kept shaking his head gently in wonder and awe, turning it in his hands, seeing new beauty in every aspect. "Sunshine is even better," she said softly, impulsively adding, "You can have that one, if you want it."

"Really?" He looked stunned.

"Sure. It needs a good home." Giving something she loved to someone who she felt might cherish it as she did was much easier than selling it to a complete stranger.

"Thank you," he said, looking at her in his intense way, as if she'd just kissed him and promised sex in the immediate future. It made her feel exposed and vulnerable and at the same time giddy and reckless.

"Mom?" Harley bellowed down the stairwell.

"What?" she snapped, embarrassed by her own emotions.

"Your sundae melted. Can I drink it?"

"Yes." Gary was still watching her. Still grateful. Still too discerning. She felt warm all over, flustered, and anxious. She started walking to the door. It was time for him to leave. "You're welcome to it, but don't let it go to your head. It doesn't mean anything."

"It means a lot to me," he said, following her when she turned out the lights and left him standing in the dark. He could take a hint. "The craftsmanship in this is remarkable. I don't think I've ever seen anything like it. I'm completely taken with it."

"That's nice," she said, waiting to say good-bye at the door. "And I'm glad if you really like it, but my giving it to you doesn't change anything. Between us, I mean. I don't want you to get any wrong ideas."

He laughed, leaning a shoulder against the wall just outside the door, facing her. "You're a thought-provoking woman, Rosemary Wickum. So maybe you should give me an example of a wrong idea."

"My life is a minor mess most of the time, and I don't have the time or the inclination to deal with another man in it. You'd be wrong to think that there could ever be anything between us but a casual friendship. That's as clear as I can be about it."

It was Gary's experience with women that if they introduced sex into the conversation before he did—even in the most roundabout fashion, it was on their minds. And if they seemed concerned about it, it was on their minds *a lot.*

"I appreciate your honesty, and the last thing I want to do is complicate your life," he said solemnly, his heart laughing wickedly as a look of surprise and disappointment flickered across her face. "Will you have dinner with me tomorrow night?"

"What?"

"I want to take you out. You won't have to deal with a thing. No cooking. No serving. No dishes to wash. You just sit there and eat. That's not complicated, is it?"

"That's not what I meant."

"Good. Is seven too late?" His gaze lowered slowly to her T-shirt and then her jeans as if he knew she had nothing else on. "Were you in for the night or getting ready to go out before?"

"No, I . . . I was in. I keep early nights."

"I'll come for you at six, then."

"No."

"Six-thirty?"

"Gary . . ."

"I'll come at six, and if you're not ready, I'll wait. I'll teach Harley some dirty garbage jokes or maybe discuss a little social reform with Earl."

That mental cartoon made her chuckle. Then she sighed. She never could hold a line when she was laughing.

"All right. Six. But I'm not getting dressed up."

"Fine. Wear your towel."

In a flash she had her finger in his face.

"I'm not getting undressed either," she told him.

His grin and the look in his eyes sent thrills and chills up the backs of her legs, up her spine, and across her scalp.

THREE

Rose had first glimpsed Justin more than two years earlier at an art auction she'd attended just for fun. She'd been too poor to actually bid on anything. She'd sat in her then best dress with her skin tingling, her heart racing, while he bid thousands of dollars for a slender, sleek piece of eye-catching art deco by a little-known artist. Curious, she'd managed to get close enough to him after the sale to ask him why he wanted that particular work. He'd said, "Deco from the twenties and thirties couldn't be touched in the seventies and eighties. I predict that by the year 2020 this piece will be worth its weight in gold. . . . That is, if gold is still worth anything by then."

His reasoning had struck her as absurd. The straight lines and modern-technology look of art deco were popular but faddish in both decades. He had no guarantee that the sculpture would be worth its weight in sand, much less gold, and yet he'd been inordinately pleased with his prize. She had determined then that he was either incredibly insightful, dumber than a barrel of hair, or he had more money than he knew what to do with.

"It's an amateur show, certainly," he was saying to her now over the phone. "But it's a place to start. Jocelyn Torpuck will have a display. . . . Of course, you have to waterproof everything she does before you can hang it in your doghouse, but her friends are good buyers. We'll spread your name around at the Arts Council affair and then again at the Patrons of Fine Arts Ball. Hopefully, people will recognize your name by show time and . . ."

"I can maybe make the Arts Council thing," she said, stretching the telephone cord from the diner's kitchen, around the coffee machine, across the pastry bar and the space behind the lunch counter to serve a BLT on whole wheat with an extra side of fries to Danny O'Brian, who owned the Ace Hardware Store three doors down. Lu had business at the bank, and Rose was tending the diner alone. "But there's no way I can afford tickets to the Patrons' Ball. What are they? Two hundred each? For cheap wine, slimy chicken, and sore feet from standing around talking to strangers who have no idea who you are and could care less? I don't think so."

"It's two-fifty this year, and if you want to make a name for yourself, you're going to have to go to these things. *You* have to make it happen. Once you start to sell, you can become an eccentric recluse. But until then, meeting the artist is half the fascination with the work—and half the buying price, I might add. I hope you're not still dreaming that someone will drive through that nowhere town, happen to see your work, buy it, and make you rich and famous. It doesn't happen like that. You have to make sacrifices. It's part of the Artist's Code or something, I'm sure. If it were easy, I'd be a billionaire by now."

"You are a billionaire."

"No, darling, only a few million. Fortunately, I have excellent taste, so it appears to be more."

"Yeah well, launching my art career this year would be pointless anyway. I won't be finished in time for the show. Not if you want to show all four at the same time."

"The three you have finished will do."

"No," she said, pouring Lucy Flannary from Lucy's Fabrics a second cup of decaffeinated coffee. Lucy was sorting through her little pillbox for her lunchtime medication. She'd forgotten her glasses at the shop again, Rose could see, and was squinting with indecision. "Lucy, these little blue pills you take at lunchtime every day," she said, casually picking one out of the wide variety of colorful pills in Lucy's box. "What are they for?"

"My stomach, honey. I take so many other pills, I need this one to keep them from eating holes in my stomach. And I have to take them with food so *they* won't eat any holes in it. I thought you knew that."

"I keep forgetting," she said.

"No what? Were you talking to me?" Justin was asking, his voice sounding irritated over the phone. He hated the constant interruptions at the diner, but he was constantly calling her there. "I wish you'd pay attention, Rose. This is your career we're talking about."

She wanted to pay attention. She really did. But at that moment the bells over the door tinkled as it opened and the King of Trash . . . er . . . Gary Albright walked in.

"What are you doing here?" she asked, happy to see him, though she wasn't sure why. He was becoming a pest.

"What?" asked Justin. "You aren't talking to me again, are you?"

"Having lunch," Gary said, smiling at her the way a starving man might a cheeseburger. "I like to eat, remember? It's one of the many things you and I have in common."

"It's the only thing we have in common," she said, tucking the receiver between her ear and her shoulder to set paper-napkin–wrapped silverware on the counter and hand him a menu. "And I can't believe you drove all the way to Redgrove to do it."

"I'd drive a lot farther if it meant seeing you again."

For crying out loud! Now he was talking like that in public. Danny and Lucy heard him, she noticed, mortified, glancing about at the other customers. Heavens above!

"The, ah, special today is meatloaf. It's good," she said, turning away, pretending she could ignore him, untangling the telephone cord as she walked back to the kitchen door. "Where were we? Yes, I'm talking to you. Oh. Right. Yes, I said no. I don't think those three are ready to show. I know what you said, but I still think they're missing something. What? No, I'm not . . . well, yes, maybe I am afraid of failure. But why bother taking that step at all if you're not going to put your best foot forward?"

"You could show the little ones. Like the one you gave me," Gary suggested in a hissing whisper to her back, boldly listening to her conversation—which in his book wasn't the same or as sneaky as eavesdropping. "They're incredible."

Rose didn't care which book he lived in, his behavior was extremely annoying. She turned to glare at him, but he had his head turned, listening to Lucy, who was saying, "She *gave* you one of her sculptures? My oh my. You hang on to it, young fellah. It's going to be worth a lot of money someday, you mark my words. We raffled one off at the Christmas bazaar this past winter at the church. We got seven hundred sixty-four dollars and fifty cents for it. It was our biggest moneymaker. I keep telling her to take some of them down to the big cities, to San Francisco or Los Angeles or even up to Portland and sell them. She could get herself a new used pickup truck. Get her old granddaddy a hearing aid. But she won't listen to nobody but that fancy art fellah," she said, and then, leaning close, she confided, "Martin, my husband, doesn't think that fellah could find his ass with both hands." She laughed. "That's what he said to me."

Rose palmed the receiver, then stuck it on her hip and growled through her teeth. "Will you two stop discussing my private affairs? They're none of your business in the first place, and in the second place, Justin just happens to own one of the most respected art galleries in San Francisco and he knows more about metallic sculpture than anyone else around and . . . and Earl doesn't need a hearing aid. The old poop hears better than I do." She ended her sentence with a jerk of her head, marking the end of her conversation and theirs.

Gary and Lucy raised their brows at each other and tried to look duly chastised. But when Gary winked his agreement to the old lady, she couldn't hold back the waggish roll of her shoulders or the upward curl of her lips.

"Justin? I'll have to call you back, my— What?" she asked, her shoulders drooping. She raised her eyes to Gary, then to Lucy and said, "Justin says he doesn't need to find his ass. He keeps his money in the breast pockets of his silk suits and to . . . to put that in your pipe and smoke it." She paused. "I know that's not what you said, but I'm not going to repeat that. Because I don't want to move to San Francisco. I like Redgrove. Look. I'll see what I can manage with the money for the Patrons' Ball, and we can talk later about showing my pieces. I have to go. Okay, I will. Bye."

"My oh my," Lucy said when Rose turned to them with thoughts of salmonella and botulism clearly on her mind. The gray-haired lady looked at her bare wrist, forgetting that she hadn't worn her watch that day. "Look at the time. I'd better get back to the shop. I need to keep an eye on Martin. He hands out all my prettiest buttons to the children if they're good while their mothers shop." She bent toward Gary again, patting his arm. "You're a nice young fellah. You can come back and eat here anytime," she said as if she owned the diner too.

"Thank you, ma'am. I will. I like the company," he said, using his grin to make her blush and titter as she walked away.

"I hope you're happy," Rose said as the bells tinkled over the door. She plopped a glass of ice water down in front of him from habit. "Justin's upset and now all of Redgrove will know I gave you one of my sculptures."

"What's wrong with that?"

"What's wrong with that? I thought you understood that I'm counting on Justin to help me show my work. He doesn't have to help me, you know. He thinks I have talent. He's been nothing but good to me and—"

"No, I meant, what's wrong with giving your sculptures away? They don't mean anything, do they? Those little ones?"

"No. Nothing. Except to me. But I don't usually give them away . . . except to certain people . . . or on special occasions."

The gratification on his face became smug and exasperating. She had to stop acting on her impulses, she decided then and there.

"What do you want?" she asked, pulling a pad and pencil from the pocket of her apron.

"You're going to write it down?"

"Yes."

"Okay." He looked thoughtful. "I suppose I want what other men want. Family. Home. Something satisfying to do with my time . . ."

"To eat."

"Oh," he said, grinning, knowing full well he was getting closer and closer to triggering her detonation. "The special, I guess. Since you recommend it."

"Drink?"

"Sure. Sometimes. Do you?"

Danny O'Brian snickered into his coffee cup at the other end of the counter and the table of four ladies behind him giggled.

"This isn't funny," she said in a harsh whisper, her hands dropping to her sides. "I work here. I have a job to do. I'm serious."

Though perhaps not as serious as she could have been, she reflected. He was so obvious in his tactics to yank her chains and get a rise out of her that it was having quite the opposite effect. She wanted to get frisky and box his ears. Light flirtation was called for, not anger. However, she'd never been any good at the former and the latter was a standard in her life—though she preferred to avoid it whenever possible.

"I can see you're serious. And I'm sorry," he said, looking far from repentant. "I'd like a very serious cup of coffee, black, when it's convenient."

It so happened to be convenient at that moment. The off-season lunch rush at Lulu's was hardly a tidal wave, and the trickle was nearly over anyway.

"You know," she said mildly, keeping her voice low as she poured his coffee. "It's a darn good thing I'm so good-natured."

"I agree. It is a good thing," he said, matching her tone of voice.

"Otherwise, I'd think you were a pain in the neck and I'd have to be sorry we ever met."

"That's true too," he said, smiling, his hazel eyes warm and bright. "But you're not, are you? Sorry that we met?"

"Not yet." Then she added pointedly, "But I have a feeling I will be."

"You can get rid of that feeling," he said. "Because once you get to know me, you're going to wonder how you ever got along without me."

"I doubt that." But she *was* beginning to suspect that he wasn't going to go away any time in the near future. "I've been muddling along on my own for a long time. And I like it that way."

"Do you like to dance?" he asked abruptly. "I forgot to ask last night. That's one of the reasons I came back today."

"You could have called to ask me that."

The animation drained from his face as he stared at her, then he grimaced, shook his head, and laughed out loud.

"It never crossed my mind," he said, self-amused. "I was too busy thinking that I wanted to see you again, I guess."

It was her turn to shake her head. He was hopeless, brain damaged from all those garbage fumes. She turned and pushed open the door to the kitchen. She went to the oven and took out the meatloaf—accidentally cutting his piece a little bigger than she'd cut the others that afternoon.

"So, what about dancing?" he called out when she

stepped in front of the window between the kitchen and the lunch counter. "Do you like to dance?"

"I don't dance." *Hadn't danced* was more the case, in thirteen . . . no, almost fifteen years. She was sure she'd forgotten how. She poured gravy into the pool of mashed potatoes on his plate.

"Well, I was trying to decide where I'd take you tonight, and there's a little jazz bar in Eureka that's nice. . . . But then I thought, if I took you dancing, I could hold you in my arms. Are you sure you don't dance?"

Her head jerked up. Danny O'Brian and the ladies at the table were eagerly awaiting her answer.

"Yes," she snapped, blushing to the tips of her ears. "Will you come back here, please," she said, setting his plate down so she could cross her arms defensively across her chest. "I want to talk to you in private."

He turned on his stool and rose to his great height, walking slowly to the end of the bar. He hadn't been behind a counter like that since college when he'd worked a part-time job at Woolworth's. Things hadn't changed much, he noticed, eager to face the encounter that awaited him in the kitchen, but feeling odd behind the lunch counter, doing nothing.

"Can I get you anything while I'm back here?" he asked, addressing the avid audience of five. "More coffee, anyone?"

They waved their hands over their cups and shook their heads and muttered polite refusals, grinning and giggling.

He shrugged and walked into the kitchen. Rose was waiting, but not patiently.

"Will you please stop acting like this," she shouted at him, though her voice was only a stern, strained whisper. "I have to live in this town, and its embarrassing to have you acting this way."

"Which way is that?" he whispered back at her. There was so much intimacy in a soft, hushed voice. And they had to stand so close to hear each other.

"Like you're in love with me. Like you can't keep your hands off me—like we've even touched in the first place. Those people out there will have us sleeping together before the night is over."

"Great."

"What?"

"I'll take all the help I can get."

"This isn't funny," she hissed. "I've already had to live down more than one scandal in this town, and I don't want to have to deal with another. I have Harley to think about, too. It's bad enough for him already. Stop this."

"If those people want to think that I'm in love with you and want to touch you, let 'em. There's nothing wrong with that. People do it all the time."

"I don't. And besides, it isn't true."

"What if it is true? What if I fell in love with you the first time I saw you? What if I want to touch you so bad, I ache?" he asked, reaching out to content himself with a light touch to her arm.

"Oh, stop." She flailed her arms, waving away his

hand, and took a step back. "You don't even know me. You don't know anything about me."

"I know me. And I know enough about you to feel the power of the possibilities between us."

"The what? Power of the possibilities? What is that? What does it mean? That you've got hot pants and I look available?"

"Not entirely," he said, undaunted. After all, where was the sense in wasting the time to deny the truth. He did want her. And in a very big way. "Possibilities come in a lot of different shapes and sizes. Bigger than sex, smaller than fear; as ordinary as common gossip, more peculiar than love. Possibilities are limitless, Rosemary. Really bad and really good, but you never know which until you try one."

"Chances," she said, redefining his possibilities. She glanced out the window again to be sure they weren't being overheard. "I have too much at risk to take chances. I won't do that to Harley."

"Or to yourself."

Okay. He had her pegged. He'd thumbed her like a magazine and found her out. She was scared. So what?

"That's right. Or to myself," she said, wanting to smash all his possibilities to smithereens; wishing he'd go away and leave her alone; hoping she could seal up the crack in the dam before it split apart and let loose all her emotions. "I took most of my chances a long time ago, and I lost. I have two left and I'm not going to screw them up." She hesitated for the briefest moment. "I've changed my mind about tonight. I appreciate the offer for dinner, but I don't think it's a good idea."

"Okay. Fine. That's it," he said, stomping out of the kitchen.

Her heart was racing and her chest was tight. She didn't like to fight and she hated hurting people . . . and she really had liked Gary. In a way. Mildly. He was a nice man. Personable. Funny, in his way. Her life wasn't his fault. He was a little overenergized, a little too intense, too full of life—sort of pushy and vigorously laboring under the false impression that she had something left in her heart to offer a man—but he wasn't a bad person.

She listened for the door of the diner to slam closed behind him as he left, but what she heard was Gary—talking to the customers.

"I'm going to take Rosemary Wickum out to dinner tonight, but before I do, I think everyone should know that despite what I want, she has no intentions of sleeping with me. Ever. And while I think that's a big mistake, it is her choice. Now, I know that you don't know who I am or where I come from, but just for the record, I would never force myself on a woman." He bowed his head humbly. "I'm a cute, sensitive type of guy, and to tell you the truth, I don't have any trouble getting women into the sack, if that's all I want." He glanced over his shoulder, knowing that Rose was listening. Her goggle-eyed expression was priceless.

"The thing is," he said, turning back to the stunned luncheoneers, "getting Rosemary into bed isn't all I want. Now, I do want to make love with her, I'm not denying that," he said, holding up one hand.

"Will you stop?"

"But I've always found sex a much more enjoyable experience if both parties are cooperating. Haven't you found this to be true?" he asked the four ladies, who ranged in age from thirty to fifty-six. They nodded, then glanced at one another self-consciously before agreeing with him again. "So, if Rosemary has no plans to cooperate with me, and if I'm too much of a gentleman to force myself on her, wouldn't you think she'd feel safe in going out with me tonight?"

"He seems okay to me, Rosie," Danny O'Brian said. He did, after all, own the hardware store, where these types of small-town judgments were decided.

"Thank you," Gary said, very man-to-man. He turned to her. "What do you say, Rosie? Won't you give me a chance to show you that I'm not such a bad guy?"

A bad guy? She was far more concerned with the fact that the man clearly didn't have both oars in the water.

However, that's not how he appeared to her neighbors. To those five apostles, who would go forth among the limited masses of Redgrove and preach the gospel truth according to Gary Albright, he looked refreshingly forthright, lovable, and sincere.

It did cross her mind to stand fast and heed her better judgment, but Lu chose that moment to return from the bank. Lu—who took to anything in pants like jelly to peanut butter, like ketchup to french fries, like syrup to waffles, like . . . well, you get the picture—was the straw that would break her back. Rose might have been able to disregard five favorable opinions, but with Lu to make the sixth, it was a lost cause.

"All right," she said finally, noting her employer's keen interest in Gary. "Dinner. Six-thirty."

"And dancing," he said, smiling. To her infuriated gasp, he shrugged and said, "You give me happy feet."

She disappeared from the window for a split second, coming out of the kitchen to meet him face-to-face behind the counter. She opened her mouth to give him fifty lashes with her sharp tongue, but nothing happened. He grinned at her.

He was the most exasperating man, yet his eyes were wondrous and full of awe when he murmured, "God, you're pretty."

What could she say?

"Oh, for pity's sake. Fine. Dinner *and* dancing. Now, will you please go?" she asked, pushing lightly on his chest. Under her breath she muttered, "I can't believe you just did that—and don't ever do it again."

"What?"

"Embarrass me like this."

"Then don't provoke me," he said simply.

"*Provoke you?*"

"I want to go out with you. I was desperate."

She sighed heavily, despairingly. "Will you please leave?"

"Aren't you forgetting something?"

"What?" she asked, her hands out as if imploring him.

He leaned forward and her heart stopped cold. Judas priest! He was going to kiss her! Right there in front of everybody! She braced herself—resisting would only make the scene worse. Her eyes grew wide and dark—in dread, of course.

Gary couldn't believe what he was seeing. He moved his face closer to hers and her lips parted in anticipation, her breath coming warm, sweet, and rapid against his. Deliberately he tilted his head to one side, looking into stormy seas of emerald green, murky with longing and need. His heart was beating hard and wild in his chest. He could . . . He would calm the stormy seas, feed the need, and grant her every wish. Later. In private. Fully. And most thoroughly.

"Rose," he murmured, their lips barely brushing. "You forgot my lunch."

FOUR

Redgrove was one of several small, New England–flavored lumber and fishing villages scattered along the rugged Pacific coastline between San Francisco and the Oregon border. Eureka being the most populated because of a choice natural harbor, and because it was the site of the world's largest redwood mills.

Redgrove was a blink and a half long. Population: six hundred and two, in the early sixties before the Redwood National Park was established. No one had bothered to change the sign since then. It was one of those tiresome and irritating little bus stops that motorists had to slow down from sixty-five to thirty-five miles per hour for, fifteen minutes before they hit the main drag —along which most of the town's residents lived.

Once upon a time, Rose had done some traveling. She called it traveling, though her intent at the time had been to run away. To escape her past, present, and future in Redgrove. But when the skyscrapers of Chicago made her lonely for the mountains and the tall redwoods, when the Arizona desert didn't smell like the ocean and the waving fields of grain on the plains of Kansas and Montana were conspicuously lacking the sound of the breakers smashing against high bluffs, she came back to Redgrove declaring "travel" to be the only valid method of learning to appreciate what you have at home.

Everyone but Earl had admired her freedom and independence, and her wisdom in "globe-trotting" while she was still young and unfettered enough to enjoy it. She'd scoffed at their definition of globe-trotting, knowing she'd seen only a small fraction of the world before she'd come crawling home. But Earl knew. Earl had answered the phone the night she'd called home crying, miserably homesick and pleading for the money to pay for a six-state bus ticket home.

To this day she couldn't regret either decision. She couldn't see the ocean from her bedroom window, but she could smell it and feel it in the moist rolling fog, and if she was very quiet—didn't even breathe—she could hear the waves pounding the rocks on the beach less than a mile away. She could stand there and feel the notion she had of being safe among the ancient redwoods, protected from behind by the snow-capped mountains, secure in the regularity of the tides. They were just the little things, of course, things she took for granted—unless she was feeling uneasy or isolated inside.

She stood there feeling exactly that, waiting for Gary. Uneasy and isolated. The sun was preparing to kiss the horizon, turning the sky mauve and magenta, as romantic as it was miraculous, as it was mysterious. She found no comfort in it.

She hadn't been out to dinner with anyone but Earl and Harley in years. She'd "done" lunch with Justin several times—in broad daylight, without dancing, without the frightened squirrels in her stomach, and without the hope that she wasn't making another huge mistake.

"Mom?" Harley's voice had been cracking like cheap china all day. It made her smile.

"What?"

"Are you ready? It's almost six-thirty."

She rolled her eyes heavenward. What a nag! Harley had been pestering her about this "big date" since she'd come home from work at four-thirty. "*Aren't you going to take a bath? Use a little extra of that stinky rose stuff. It smells nice.*" "*You're not wearing jeans, are you? He's gonna think there's something wrong with your legs. Don't you have* anything *with a skirt on it?*" "*Would it kill you to use some lipstick or something?*"

"Yes, Harley, I'm ready to go."

"Get out of the window," he said, appearing in the doorway—for a final inspection no doubt. "He'll think you're watching for him."

"I am."

"Well, don't. And I'll get the door when he gets here." He stepped into the room, eyeing her attire. "Nothing shorter, huh?"

"Harley," she said, half shocked, looking down at the hem of her short denim skirt. She could already feel a breeze on her fanny. How much shorter did he want it? "Women my age begin to have sagging body parts, you know. If this were any shorter, my bottom would hang out."

"You still have nice legs. Can't hurt to show 'em off a little."

"You think so?" she asked, checking for herself, inordinately flattered by her son's praise. Her *son's* praise, it occurred to her. "You know, I don't think other sons would be encouraging their mothers to wear shorter skirts for some man they hardly know. What is it with you and this dinner? You weren't invited, you know."

"I know," he said, looking young and shy for a second. "I've just never seen you go out with anyone before." He shrugged. "I mean, I was thinking about it . . . and, well, I asked Grampa. He said you hadn't been out with a man since . . . my dad. How come?"

She looked away to consider her answer, moving slowly toward the bed to sit down. "No interest, I guess. It was hard to trust men after your dad, and then later, when you were little and I was working at the plant, I was too busy and too tired to have much of an interest in men."

"Was it because of me? Because I didn't have a dad? Because men don't want women with kids?"

"No," she said without hesitation.

"I remember men coming to the house, asking you out. But you never went with them."

"I didn't want to. It had nothing to do with you." A brief pause. "As I recall, most of them would follow you home from somewhere or another, telling me what a great kid you were. That little league coach you had made me really nervous. I kept thinking that if you ever came up missing, he'd have kidnapped you. Your third grade teacher was the same way."

"So, how come you didn't date 'em?"

"I told you. I didn't want to."

"Why?"

"I don't know," she said, frowning, feeling annoyed for no good reason in particular. "It was easier that way." She laughed. "Men think women are weird, but it's really the other way around. You're just a young man, but you're getting weirder every day."

"Don't you get lonely?" he asked. His green eyes that were so like her own were solemn and grave. Even as a small child he'd had these profoundly thoughtful moments when he seemed like a very wise, very troubled old man trapped in a kid's innocence.

"I have you. And Grampa," she said, a standard mother's answer that clearly didn't satisfy him. She knew what he was asking, and he knew it. "I do get lonely. Sometimes. It passes. And then I'm glad it's just you and me and Earl."

"It won't be forever, you know," he said, reminding her that both he and Earl were getting older. They both listened to a car coming to a slow stop out front.

"I'll deal with that then," she said, rising to her feet. "In the meantime I'm happy with things the way they are, so you can stop trying to pawn me off on some unsuspecting man. Okay?"

He grinned, looking to savvy by far. "I don't think this guy is unsuspecting, Mom."

The squirrels were awake and clawing at her insides again.

"He is a little obvious, isn't he?"

"Lu said he could have lit up a neon sign this afternoon in the diner."

"He could have lit up Las Vegas," she muttered when he left the room to answer the knock at the door downstairs. She felt a fresh wash of mortification recollecting the moment she'd realized he wasn't going to kiss her right there behind the lunch counter. The unexpected disappointment had been staggering, and he'd grinned when it showed on her face. "The jerk."

He didn't deserve all the trouble she'd gone to, shaving her legs and putting on makeup. She pulled the carefully tucked cotton blouse from the waistband and knotted the tails in front so he wouldn't think she cared how she looked. Then she frowned down on the little black smudge across the toe of the white sneakers she'd put on, hoping she'd feel lighter on her feet when the time came.

This was exactly why she didn't date. A lot of trouble and fuss for nothing. She'd mention this to Harley tomorrow, she decided, walking into the living room.

"Look, Mom. Flowers," Harley said, grinning, indicating the clay pot in Gary's hands. One leaf and a thin green stub of a stem protruded from the center of it. "Eventually."

"It's a refugee," Gary told her, his expression announcing his delight in seeing her again. "A little love and kindness, and it'll be a red begonia someday."

How appropriate.

Rose tucked her tongue into her cheek and graciously accepted the near dead vegetation without comment—however, both Harley and Gary saw the amusement in her eyes and knew it was a favorable omen.

He hadn't been sure of the reception he'd get. Earlier she had thrust his plate of meatloaf into his hands and promptly disappeared into the kitchen while he ate. His new friend Danny O'Brian had passed him some meaningful glances in relation to the amount of noise she'd made with the pots and pans, but she hadn't even said good-bye when he left.

Rose set the grocery store reject in the kitchen window where it could catch the morning sun—and where she might remember to water it once in a while. She took a moment to collect herself.

She didn't want to enjoy Gary Albright or his silly sense of humor. She didn't want to like him or the pleasurable feelings he stirred in her. She was determined not to have a good time in his company. Let's face it, what woman in her right mind, who wasn't looking for a relationship in the first place, would choose to go out with a garbageman?

Hmmm. On the other hand, who else would she go out with? Who would be safer? Now, that was a consoling thought. If she started to feel the slightest bit attracted to him, all she had to do was remind herself that he was a garbageman.

Not that there was anything wrong with garbagemen as a whole, mind you. And she was sure there was an auxiliary association of garbagemen's wives somewhere too. She simply wasn't interested in joining.

"You have plenty of gas?" she heard Harley asking.

"Yes, sir," Gary answered, playing along good-naturedly.

"I want her home in time to fix my lunch for school tomorrow. Is that understood?"

"Yes, sir."

She watched Harley slip an arm around her date's shoulder and turn him away, speaking in hushed tones. Her face burned hot as a torch when Gary nodded another "yes, sir" and patted the wallet in his rear pants pocket with his hand.

"Harley, honey," she said, taking his hand to lead him away, refusing to hear Gary's chuckle, avidly avoiding the expression on his face. She led her only son back to the kitchen, muttering, "You will not live to see morning." Adding in a louder voice, "Don't forget that you need to cook supper for you and Grampa. I left the directions there on the counter. Follow them."

An inch or two taller than she, he bent his head to her and whispered, "Do you have a quarter in your sock . . . just in case?"

She stuck a finger in his face and wordlessly told him that he'd crossed the line. By several miles.

He grinned. "Try to have fun," he whispered with an impulsive peck to her cheek.

"You are the worst son I've ever had, but I love you anyway," she told him.

"Yo, Gary," he said, turning away from her. "Remember what I told you, man."

"Yes, sir."

Rose sighed a mother's sigh and reached for her purse.

"He's only been a teenager for a year and a half and already it feels like a lifetime."

"Wait till he starts driving," he said, smiling as she groaned. "Earl, as always, it's been a pleasure talking with you. I hope to see you again soon."

Rose wasn't aware that they'd exchanged even a single word, but the old man lifted a friendly hand and waved them good-bye—or waved them away from in front of the television set, she wasn't sure which.

He followed her down the stairs and out of the front door of the gas station to where he'd parked his truck. If her truck were a blueberry buggy, his would have been a sumptuous sapphire carriage—with powder blue custom accents and shiny chrome trim.

"I have a car but . . . not with me. I hope you don't mind."

"No, I don't mind."

"Wait a second, let me get that," he said as she reached out to open the door.

"Look," she said, feeling ridiculous. "I can open doors for myself. You don't have to go to all this rigmarole for a simple dinner. I know you're trying to be nice, but it really isn't necessary."

"Yes, it is."

"No. It isn't."

"Yes, it is," he said again, reaching into the truck and removing another clay pot. "I didn't want you to sit on this. I had to special order it." He held it out to her. "This is for you. The other one was to amuse the kid."

"Thank you," she said, taking the shrubby little plant. The leaves were tiny and intensely green, and there were little blue flowers scattered among them. It smelled wonderful. A sharp, sweet, sort of minty smell. "I don't think I've seen this before. It's very pretty."

"Yes, it is."

"What is it?"

"Rosemary." She looked up and could tell immediately that he wasn't talking about the plant.

"Like rosemary and thyme?"

He nodded. "I looked it up. One of the books said it was native to the Mediterranean. Only the leaves are used for seasoning, you know, but extracts from the flowers are used in medicines and perfumes." He touched one with the tip of his finger. "In *Hamlet*, Ophelia says, 'There's rosemary, that's for remembrance.' But in the language of flowers it means fidelity in love. I like both meanings, don't you?"

"Yes. I do," she said, semistunned that he'd gone to such lengths with her name.

"In another book they said it was sometimes called sea-dew, too, and that it's useful in lovemaking. . . ." He frowned in concentration. "That had something to do with Venus, the love goddess, springing from the foam of the sea and the sea-dew helping to express sexual love." He laughed. "The book didn't say whether you were supposed to eat it, rub it on, or shake it at the moon, so I didn't try it. But, all in all, it sounded like a nifty little plant to give to someone named Rosemary."

"It sure does," she said, charmed. "I mean, it is. Thank you. For thinking of it and for . . ." She didn't know what else she wanted to thank him for. Everything, she supposed. For the plant. For looking up the meaning of Rosemary. For asking her out. For putting up with her freakish foibles. For his freakish foibles, too, she supposed, since she was feeling kindly toward him at that moment.

". . . for not giving away the plant's secrets in front of Harley," he said, filling in the blank for her, standing away from the door so she could get in. "He'd have that sucker plucked clean in no time."

She laughed, and he swung the door closed, then she grimaced as if in pain. They hadn't pulled out of the drive and already the date wasn't going well. She was having fun.

"Now, if you don't like the place I've picked out, you let me know," he said, taking Highway 101 north toward Arcata, a twenty-minute drive from Redgrove. "I was amazed at how many nice places there were to choose from around here. Thank God for tourism, or I'd have had to take you to one of those seedy waterfront places I was in this afternoon."

Ah-ha!

"You were down there drinking all afternoon?" she asked with a practiced calm.

Though he didn't look any worse for the wear, it was mildly gratifying to know that she hadn't misjudged him. She'd suspected that first day that he was a heavy drinker, and it certainly explained a great deal of his behavior.

"Not drinking, just looking around."

Oh.

"At what?" she asked, chagrined. "The fishing boats?"

"A few. Mainly I was checking out bars and chowder houses."

"For what?"

"For food and a dance floor."

"You mean you . . ." She turned her head and tried to read the expression on his face by the dash lights. Surely he was funning with her again. "You spent the afternoon looking for a place to take me tonight?"

"Well, if this were Sacramento or Fairfield or San Francisco, I'd know where to take you. But I don't go out much when I'm up here."

"Why didn't you ask me to recommend a place?"

"I was afraid you'd say Burger King and end our date at seven-thirty."

She smiled, inside and out. Granted, her dates with eligible men had been few and far between, but she couldn't recall anyone going to such pains to ensure her having a good time. In fact, she couldn't remember anyone at any time going to such pains to ensure her having anything.

"So, where do you stay when you're up here?" she asked, needing a change of subject.

"I have a little place outside Eureka. A property investment really. Not much there but a roof and a bed."

"How long do you usually stay?"

"Depends. A week. Sometimes two. Longer if I need to. Less if I don't. I keep a flexible schedule so I can drop in unexpectedly and check things out. Ride the trucks. Go over the books. I get a better picture that way."

"You actually ride on the back of the garbage trucks?"

"Now and again. I don't want to forget what it's like out there. And it gives me a chance to see my guys in action. Make sure they're putting the lids back on the cans."

"You really love being a garbageman, don't you?"

"Yep," he said, turning his blinker on to take a left-hand turn to Arcata. "No sense in working hard at something you can't care about. Even Harley knows that."

They glanced at each other across the bench seat, silently debating the issue.

"Harley doesn't want to understand," she said, looking out the window at the settling dusk. "It's only temporary."

"How'd you get interested in welding?"

"I grew up with it. In the garage."

"You grew up over the gas station?"

"Earl was a lumberjack most of his life. Before the fight to save the redwoods. My dad was a teenager when Earl got pinned under one of them and broke his back. He bought into the gas station as an independent dealer with the insurance money and every dime of his savings and he . . . he and my dad worked it until . . . Well, the oil embargoes in the seventies and eighties were hard on all the independents."

"So your family stayed on and you started building art in the garage?"

"Eventually," she said, uncomfortable with the details of her childhood. "I was a welder at a chain-link fence factory up until three years ago. When it closed down, Lu, ah, Lulu gave me a job, and that's when I started the bigger sculptures. The little ones were for fun. A hobby. Just something I enjoyed doing."

He thought about reiterating the differences between the sculptures she loved and those she was doing because she felt she had to, but decided to let Harley do it and stay out of it. He had her talking to him, and there was so much more he wanted to know about her.

He'd chosen Bill's BBQ Bar and Grill not for the originality of its name but for its menu and atmosphere. It was perched on a pier overlooking the water and had soft lights and tablecloths. Not much, but nothing to spit at in this neck of the woods. And Rose could order anything she wanted, from spaghetti to fish to steak.

Choice had been important. And only because he sensed that Rose hadn't had, didn't have, or wouldn't allow herself to have too many choices. It was just a feeling he couldn't shake, despite the fact that she was a tough little cookie who knew her own mind and wasn't afraid to voice it. She was an odd combination of reserved and straightforward, an intriguing mixture of compliant and rigid, and he wanted to know why.

"Lu's been to every restaurant within a hundred miles of Redgrove. She's our local expert. She says it's to check out the competition, but she just likes to eat. I think she said this place had great food," Rose said, looking around, feeling horribly underdressed even though denim seemed to be part of the dress code.

It better have great food, Gary thought, amazing himself at how much he wanted to impress her. Their gazes caught above the menus and she smiled, but he could see she was uncomfortable.

"This isn't a great place, is it?" he asked, leaning across the table and speaking softly. "We can go somewhere else."

She bent over her menu to whisper back. "Don't you like it? I've never been anywhere as nice, but if you want to go somewhere else . . ."

"No, no. I like it fine. I just thought you . . . well, you look a little uneasy."

She smiled and lowered her eyes away from his.

"I am," she admitted, looking back at him. "I don't do this very often. I'm afraid I'll spill something."

"You don't eat out?" Where had she been all her life?

"Sure I do. Every chance I get. At Lu's or McDonald's. Not in nice places like this and not with . . ."

"Not with what?"

"A date. A man."

His smile was slow in coming to his lips, as his body was suddenly tingling with excitement. Her confession aroused a sweet ache inside him. He'd never had better news.

"Don't worry about spilling. If you do, I'll spill something, too, and then we'll both look stupid. How's that?"

She laughed softly. "I'll be careful."

His hesitation to say more was so brief, she hardly noticed it.

"As to your being here with me, I guess I could probably tell you not to think of me as a real date . . . or as a man, but then I'd be at cross-purposes, wouldn't I?"

A trick question, she decided, and left it unanswered.

"Tell me about your furnace," she said hastily.

"My furnace?"

"The thing you're building that's making everyone mad."

"Oh," he said, leaning back to relax in the arms of the chair.

The waitress came before he could start. He ordered salmon and Rose asked for flounder.

"Would you like wine?"

"Wine?"

"To drink with dinner?"

"No, the water's fine, thanks. But you go ahead."

"You don't drink." It was a statement.

The waitress was walking away. Rose shook her head slowly and bowed her head.

"My dad drank enough for both of us," she said impulsively, instantly regretting it. What would he think of her now? Not that she cared, she reminded herself, then added fuel to the fire. "He drank himself to death, in fact."

"I'm sorry."

He *was* sorry. She could see it in his eyes. There was sorrow and something else. It was as if he understood that it hadn't been her fault, that it had nothing to do with her, that the sins and diseases of the father weren't always delivered on the children.

"My mom died in a car accident when I was nine and . . . and my dad got worse than ever after that. Earl was more of a father to me."

"Does he ever talk?" he asked with enough insight into her growing years to know that dredging them up would spoil her evening.

"When he wants something," she said, smiling. "He likes you."

"He told you that?"

"Of course not. But he does recognize your comings and goings. Harley and I just sort of fade in and out of his peripheral vision while he's watching TV. He saves up his requests for when we happen to pass by."

"Was he always like that?"

"Pretty much," she said, fondness softening her expression. "He likes to pretend he's deaf so we won't bother him, but he's always the first to show up when we need him."

"That's when it counts," he said, wanting to dig further and further into her life. Aware, suddenly, that *he* wanted to be the one to show up when she needed someone. "And what about Harley's father? Where is he?"

She shrugged indifferently. "I have no idea."

"He doesn't help out?"

"Why should he?" Gary looked startled. "Harley was my choice. He left some money to help pay for the abortion, but . . ." She shrugged again. Harley was the best decision she'd ever made, and nothing else about him mattered.

"I thought you were divorced," he said, more to himself than to her, recalling finally that Earl, Rose, and Harley all had the same last name. It had explained her reluctance to get involved with another man. Being an unwed mother would explain it, too, but . . . "You were young."

"Not so very. I was nineteen," she said, and then because talking to him was as easy as slipping on ice, she added, "I'd run away from home twice by then."

Gary was starting to feel punchy. He hadn't dreamed he'd be opening such a huge can of worms. She was by far a much stronger woman than he'd imagined. Her life made his seem like a picnic—and it pretty much had been, he thought. If the worst things that ever happened to him as a kid were being called garbage boy because his dad rode on the back of a sanitation truck and having to endure endless jokes about the origins of everything he'd ever owned, then his childhood *had* been a picnic.

"Why?" he asked, feeling nosy and half afraid she'd be offended and not answer, but asking anyway.

"Why what?"

"Why'd you run away from home?"

"Well, Redgrove looks a lot better to me now than it did in those days. Back then I thought it was hell on earth. Everyone knew everyone else's business. My mother was gone. My dad was a drunk. And Earl . . . Earl said I could do anything I wanted to do, if I wanted to do it bad enough. So I left."

"Just like that?"

She nodded and smiled at her foolishness. "I was fifteen the first time. I hitched to San Francisco. It only took a week to spend all the money I'd saved while I was looking for a job. But who was going to give a scrawny little kid a job? The second time, I was seventeen and a half and calling myself eighteen. I worked truck stops and bars where it was legal, from here to Chicago."

"Why'd you come back?"

"I was homesick . . . and pregnant with Harley. Earl sent me bus fare. He always has money stashed around somewhere."

"Was your dad alive then? When you came home?"

"Oh, yeah. Between the two of us, Redgrove was a regular soap opera for a while."

"He was mad? About Harley? And your running away?"

"No, not really," she said passively. "He just made sure that I knew that Earl's disability check couldn't handle another mouth, much less two more, and he went on drinking. That's when I went to work at the fence factory."

Gary stared at her for a long moment, then glanced away, shaking his head. "You sound so impervious to it all."

"Do I?" she asked, searching inward. "Maybe I am now, to parts of it. It's been a long time, and things have changed. And it was a long time before I noticed that not everyone was growing up the way I was. I didn't know it was supposed to be different." She smiled. "What about you? You grew up wanting to be a garbageman. That must have been a surprise to your teachers."

As it happened, nothing Gary did ever surprised his teachers. His older brother had paved a path for him at school—so his dreams of becoming a trashman weren't unheard of—and it wasn't long before his teachers and friends received their first few injections of his shocking personality, which soon came to be expected rather than startling.

He was a surprise to Rose, however. Constantly. The next few minutes included.

He was almost timid in telling her about growing up between his two brothers with a mother who made sure he washed behind his ears and ate his lima beans, and a father who spent years coaching junior league football after work. And he could hardly look her in the eye when he disclosed that his mother had taken a job and his father had worked an extra four nights a week as a janitor to get them through college.

"They just had their forty-fifth wedding anniversary a few months ago," he said, finishing off the last of the wine in his glass. "We got together and gave them cruise tickets. That's where they are now, somewhere in the Caribbean, buying souvenirs for Christmas presents."

"And having a wonderful time," she said, warming to the affection in his voice when he spoke of his family. She didn't think it was fair to envy him his parents, but she couldn't help hoping that maybe someday Harley's eyes and voice would be soft and gentle when he spoke of her.

"You're staring at me," he said, uncommonly self-conscious.

"I'm amazed."

"By what?"

"By what a sweet man you are."

"Sweet?" he asked, pretending to have a bitter taste in his mouth, making believe that he couldn't feel the uncomfortable warmth seeping into his cheeks. "I spend days trying to sweep you off your feet with my all-male charm and studly physique, and you're amazed by sweet?"

"Those are pretty amazing, too," she said, her gaze wandering across his broad chest and straight, thick shoulders; lifting to his mouth and then his eyes once more. "But sweet gets to me."

It would have been the wine talking, she thought, if she'd had any. It had to be the night. The excitement. It would wear off and tomorrow she wouldn't care if his heart were made of pure cane sugar from Hawaii.

"Well, getting to you is my prime objective here, so . . . sweet it is," he said in his best debonair voice. He gave her a libertine look. "Would you like something *sweet* for dessert?"

She chuckled. "I couldn't eat another mouthful."

"Hmmm. You like sweet, and I love women who talk dirty. We were made for each other," he said, teasing her, his eyes hooded, a sly smile on his lips.

Dirty? Her? What had she said?

"Oh! No, I didn't mean—I thought you meant . . ."

He started to laugh. "I'm sorry," he said, realizing

her defenses were displaced. "But you walked right into that one, and I have no self-control. Would you like some coffee?"

"No," she said thoughtfully, enjoying the relaxed, untroubled calm inside her and reluctant to disturb it by getting rewired with coffee. "But maybe some fresh air. Could we walk a little?"

Perfect. Gary loved it when a plan came together.

FIVE

The ocean had a way of fooling people into thinking it was something gentle and benevolent. Slow lapping waves lulled you into forgetting that the water could rise up and swallow you whole. Unseasonably hot spring days deceived you, allowing you to hope that the evenings would be warm as well, but they never were.

"Take my brother's operation as an example," he was saying as he removed the sport coat he'd worn over a cable knit sweater and jeans. "He can pull off enough methane gas from three million tons of garbage to meet the needs of eighteen thousand homes for the next fifteen years." He held out his coat and waited for her to slip her arms into the sleeves. "Huge underground pockets of methane gas, just sitting there waiting to explode or leak into the atmosphere and destroy the ozone."

"So you think these waste-to-energy programs are

the answer to pollution," she said, tingling as her muscles uncoiled in the warmth left in his jacket.

By the lapels, he turned her to him and began to button her in. "I think they could be part of the answer, yes. A small part."

"Then why are people so upset about your incinerator?"

"They don't understand it. All they know is that burning garbage has been banned in this country for the last fifty years." He took hold of one arm, then the other, rolling up the jacket sleeves. "And rightly so. The old furnaces released dioxin and acid gases into the air."

"Those cause cancer, right?"

"Among other things," he said, casually slipping his hand around hers as they walked on, heading north as if by random choice. "But the new ones burn hotter; even glass and pottery melt and crumble. For every ten truckloads of garbage, there will be one full of ash to bury."

"So, where's the energy?" she asked, going over it in her mind. "Didn't you say it was a waste-to-energy thing . . . or is burning the trash down to ash considered energy saving?"

"No, no. The incinerator will be an energy source," he said, pleased to explain to her. "Water, running through rows of pipes on all sides of the furnace, picks up the heat and eventually expands into a powerful steam. That's channeled through more pipes to keep an electrical generator spinning, like a steam engine."

"So the incinerator produces enough energy to run itself."

"Itself and seventy-five hundred homes. Indefinitely."

"So, what's the problem?" she asked, her ears picking up country western music from a tavern on the roadway above them. "Why don't you explain it to everyone the way you have to me? Send out pamphlets or something."

"We will, but it won't matter."

"Why not? I think it's a great idea."

"Aesthetics," he said, using a simple word she'd understand.

"Aesthetics? Well, plant some bushes around it. Paint it purple. If you can make electricity from garbage, surely you can think of some way to dress up the incinerator so it isn't an eyesore."

"Should I paint the trucks too? Or borrow a Klingon cloaking device so no one can see or hear them driving up and down the road? How about if I hose them down with fancy perfume from Paris every time they pull into the yard so they won't offend anyone?"

She grimaced, though she knew his irritation wasn't with her. "People are that picky? Even with all the good it will do?"

"The incinerator site is seven miles from the housing development, and all they can talk about is the smell and what the trucks sound like and what'll happen if the pollution control devices break down."

"What would happen?"

"We'd shut down and fix them. And you can bet your last nickel those emission control people will know exactly when it happens. They're closing down everything that even hints at a leak these days."

"And that's good, right?"

"The idea is to help, not to make things worse. I'd rather detect a malfunction before it happens. But if I don't, I'd want them to shut me down."

"What are you going to do? Can they stop you from building it?"

"They can waste more time and money in courtrooms, but in a few years it won't matter. While they're busy fighting me, someone else will build an incinerator seven miles off in the other direction. You can't stop the future. Especially if it makes sense, and if you've run out of time and choices."

"And we have, haven't we? With the pollution and all?"

"I'm afraid so. We have to do something now or it'll be too late." He stopped and gravely added, "Fortunately, there's still time for us to dance. Do you know how to line dance?"

"What?" It was a second or two, as he pulled her toward the stairs that led up to the road, before she realized what he meant. "No. I told you I don't dance. I was hoping you'd changed your mind."

"Are you kidding? Come on. We can learn together then," he said, starting up the steep steps ahead of her, her hand wrapped tightly in his. "This place isn't too bad for a honky-tonk and—"

He was jerked backward when she stopped suddenly behind him.

"You checked this place out. I . . . I walked into this one, too, didn't I?"

He smiled sympathetically and nodded.

"You were bringing me here all along."

"Five minutes. If you hate it, we'll leave." To distract her, he looked up suddenly, searching the eastern sky, then seemed surprised when he said, "Oh, look there. See those three stars there, lined up in a row?" He continued up the steps as he spoke. She followed blindly, gazing heavenward. "That's the belt of Orion, the hunter. You can't see Canis Major from here, but down a little and farther east is Canis Minor, and ah . . . there, there in the nose of Canis is Procyon, the brightest star in the sky."

They'd reached the top of the cliff and the paved parking lot where, by day, tourists parked to treasure the view, snap photographs, and reevaluate their decisions not to practice some sort of religion.

"You know about stars?" she asked, searching for Procyon, picking out three or four good candidates.

"I told you I was a really bright guy, that I went to college and everything."

She could feel him looking at her, watching her.

"You can't usually see this many stars because of the fog," she said, smiling. "Lucky for you it's a clear night, or you wouldn't be able to show off like this."

He laughed, gently guiding her toward the Rio Rider. "You ain't seen nothin' yet, lady. I have more talent and smarts in my little finger"—he showed it to her—"than most men have in their whole body."

"And yet you're so humble."

"I know. I can't help that either."

She knew what he was doing. Talking circles around her until he could get her inside the Rio Rider. She could still say no. She could put her foot down and insist he take her home. But she didn't. She didn't even want to.

The music outside was a muffled hum compared to the noise that nearly knocked them over at the door. Happy, snappy noise that quickened her heartbeat and stroked something very young inside her.

Fingers entwined, because he wouldn't release them, they stood near the bar, gauging the crowd, watching the dancers, and looking for a table to sit at.

It wasn't as big as some places she'd seen, years before. There was a small stage and dance floor, cluttered tables everywhere, pool tables and video games far off to one side. But the atmosphere was familiar—smoke, dim lights, colored neon signs, a cheerful hum of voices, feet shuffling and hands clapping to loud recorded music.

"Well, as I live and breathe, will you look who's here?" a familiar voice exclaimed.

"Lu!"

"I can't believe my eyes. I thought for sure you'd lock yourself in the bathroom and refuse to go out tonight. It's like I've been saying all along, all it takes is the right man," she said, laying her hand on Gary's free arm and looking up to adore him. "That must be you, honey."

"Now you both think so," Rose said, delighted to have an ally on foreign soil. Lu was wearing a red silk blouse with western fringe, too-tight black jeans, and a black hat. Lu knew how to dress. "What are you doing here?"

"Boot-scootin' my butt off, same as you. Come on. You can sit at our table."

"Lu," she shouted over the loud music, following her because she had Gary in tow. "Who are you here with?"

Lu swung around into her face and yelled, "Jimmy Dusom, and he's doin' some for me." She threw her head back and enjoyed her own pun. "He just got back yesterday. He's going to work one of his dad's fishing boats all summer. Oh, I know, I know. He's young enough to be my . . . my distant cousin or something, but he turned twenty-one last winter. He's fair game. And he has the most incredible tush. Wait till you see it."

Rose gave her a closed-lip smile and refused to make any judgments. She liked Lu. There was only a year difference in their ages, but she was several inches taller and that made her seem much older than Rose. She'd appeared in Redgrove about ten years earlier, after her fourth divorce. Right away she was labeled as friendly, then very friendly, with an occasional lifted eyebrow. But no one seemed to expect anything different of Lu. They accepted her as she was—blunt, rowdy, and sexually active.

And yet, instinctively, you knew there was more to Lu's book than her cover.

For instance, in four marriages no children had been produced and still she had readily and generously agreed to care for Harley if anything ever happened to Rose. She doted on young customers, fussing over them, giving them free ice cream, dropping maraschino cherries and little paper umbrellas into their soft drinks.

Also, she never dated any man she couldn't control. She might flirt with the likes of Gary, but she dated pliable young men or older, less-spirited men. Never anyone her equal.

Lu never reminisced aloud about the days before she came to Redgrove, and Rose never asked, because she had a powerful suspicion they hadn't been pleasant.

"Jimmy, you remember Rose from the diner? And this huge hunk of heaven is Gary," Lu said, making introductions without last names. Jimmy was a tall, thin, clean-cut youth who had the overwhelmed expression of a child with the keys to a candy store. The men shook hands, and Lu pushed Gary into the chair next to hers, so he shoved the chair between him and Jimmy out for Rose. "You're going to love this place," she hollered. "In the summer they have a live band and this place rocks."

Gary leaned forward in his chair to talk into Rose's ear.

"If the kid starts to foam at the mouth, should I shoot him?" he asked, his voice tickling along her neck.

She laughed and shook her head, moving her cheek up against his. "Nah. I think Lu'll put him down before he bites anyone but her."

They laughed into each other's eyes, sharing more than the humor and more than an easy tolerance of those around them. An understanding of friendship, like-thinking, and appreciation passed between them.

"Would you like a beer or something else to drink?" he asked, his nose in her hair.

"A diet soda would be nice."

"You smell good."

She pulled away, looking at him as if to say he'd sniffed illegally. But the expression on his face told her to beware, he was a born outlaw and would commit any crime that presented itself. It pleased him. He craved it.

He turned and bellowed to Lu, making a circle with his finger above the table. Then he pushed back his chair and stood up, saying to Rose, "I'm going after drinks. Can I get you anything else?"

She shook her head and smiled and heard Lu tell him, "You said you wanted someplace clean. You didn't say anything about great service," and started to laugh.

She waited for him to walk away before moving into his chair and all but stood on her head to drag Lu's attention from Jimmy.

"What did you mean, just then, that he wanted someplace clean?"

"He asked me about a nice place to go dancing. At the diner this afternoon," she said. Giving her a sharp look, she added, "When you weren't being very nice to him. He asked me if I could scrounge up a date and meet you here. He thought you'd be more comfortable and have more fun with people you knew."

Rose looked away, uncertain of what to think, very certain of the aching inside her. She looked up again when Lu's hand came to rest on her arm, squeezing gently, reassuringly.

"He's a good man, Rosie. They don't make many like him, honey."

Maybe. Maybe not, she thought, her stomach a knot of turmoil she wasn't ready to untie yet. Why did he have to be so nice? She turned her gaze from Lu's keen scrutiny to watch the dancers, two by two, spinning and stepping in time to the music.

What was she doing here? She'd never be able to dance like that, she decided, allowing her mind to wander, refusing to contemplate the merits and failings of good men at that moment. As if she wanted any sort of man in her life, for crying out loud. What good was a good man? What exactly was it they were good for? She picked out an older couple to watch because of their grace and agility and familiarity with each other when they danced. They'd probably been dancing together for a hundred years, she guessed, thinking it sweet; wondering if the old gentleman was a good man; envying them someplace deep in her soul.

"What did you say he did for a living?" Lu asked, patting her arm to get her attention.

"I don't think I said." Oh, Lord. She was about to become a member of the Joke-of-the-Month Club.

"Well? What does he do?"

"Lots of things. This and that."

"Like what?"

"Environmental stuff. Pollution. He's got degrees in biology and chemistry. Environmental science too."

Lu tipped her head to one side to look over her

shoulder at Gary by the bar. She sighed wistfully. "Well, he's somethin', honey."

Something for sure.

She felt a nudge at her shoulder and turned, expecting to see Gary.

"Wanna dance?" asked a man she'd never laid eyes on. A big burly fellow with a nice face and a friendly smile.

She wavered, surprised to be noticed and singled out, afraid of looking foolish on the dance floor, unsure of modern dating etiquette.

She was saved a decision when a frowning Gary appeared behind the man, holding three beer bottles in one hand and a glass of dark liquid in the other. She motioned for the man to beware and not to back into him, maybe step aside so Gary could unburden himself, but he took it as a refusal to dance.

"Sorry, man," he said to Gary, smiling back at Rose.

Gary wanted to drop-kick him, but said instead, "No problem, big fellah," and sat down beside her.

"I feel so sorry for me," he said, leaning toward her to be heard, playing pathetic.

"Why?"

"Because no man wants to be the guy with the prettiest woman in a place like this. You end up fighting for her all night and missing teeth in the morning."

He was teasing her again. Wasn't he? He wasn't laughing. He looked at the tables around them. He was going too far now, she thought, also looking around, just in time to see a couple of male heads turn away from them. Well, that didn't mean anything. Lu, after all, was something to see.

There was hardly enough time to take a breath between the end of one song and the beginning of the next, she noticed, when the tempo and rhythm of the music changed. The Rio Rider was not a good place for talking.

"Come on, you two. Don't just sit there," Lu said, jumping up and dragging Jimmy to his feet.

"Lu, I can't do those dances. I can't do that," she told Gary. "We'll watch, okay?"

"No way," Lu said, releasing Jimmy and taking hold of her hands. "This is a line dance and you're going to learn it. Come on, I'll teach you." She waved to Gary. "I'll teach you both. It's fun. You'll love it."

Love it? Well, they had a grand time screwing up. Leading with the wrong foot, bumping into the real dancers and messing up the line. They liked sticking their fingers in their pockets with the thumbs hanging out and trying again and again and again to stay in line, laughing hilariously when they couldn't, attempting to walk away and being pulled back into the column by complete and very forgiving strangers.

Love it? Well, they enjoyed being a part of the crowd, and the crowd seemed to acknowledge that they were a twosome. They looked forward to the music coming to an abrupt silence and a slow, soft song taking its place, to moving into each other's arms and swaying gently. No fancy footwork required.

Love it? Well, a few hours later they collapsed

flushed, exhausted, and happy into chairs and gulped greedily on fresh cold drinks.

"I love that," she said, laughing, placing her soda-cooled palms to her cheeks. "I think we've almost got it, Gary. We hardly missed a step this time." The smile faded from her lips. "What's wrong?"

He offered her a weak smile and looked away as if he were suddenly shy and awkward.

"What?"

"Nothing," he said, words failing him. It didn't happen to him often, but it did happen.

"Are you sure?"

How could he tell her what he couldn't explain? How could he tell her that she was so beautiful, she took his breath away? How could he tell her that when she laughed, he thought his heart might explode? How could he tell her that when her eyes were bright and shiny and full of happiness, he could see his life looking back at him?

"Positive. Are you getting tired? I don't want your boss to get mad if you're dragging tomorrow."

They looked at Lu, twirling on the end of Jimmy's arms, and happened to catch her eye. When Jimmy passed her behind him, she pointed out his remarkable tush and started to giggle.

"I don't think my boss is going to notice if I even show up tomorrow," she said fondly, turning back to Gary. "But maybe we should go. I don't want Harley to worry."

"Think he will?"

She smiled, recalling his earlier behavior. "Probably not."

George Strait's "Last in Love" started up on the jukebox.

"Last dance," he said, standing and holding a hand out to her.

Of course, she didn't know George Strait from B.B. King without an announcement. All she knew was that he had a nice mellow voice, and dancing in Gary's arms was something she could do forever. She could rest her head on his broad shoulder, close her eyes, hear nothing in her head but the music, feel nothing but the gentle pressure of his embrace.

Best of all, she wasn't thinking of tripping or bumping into anyone or falling down. Gary was there. He'd catch her. And her sense of security went beyond physical accidents. Emotional bumps and ego bruises. Gary was there. He'd bandage them, let her lean on him until she was strong again. She knew these things about him instinctively, and, yet, in the back of her mind lurked the question, how long? How Long? HOW LONG?

Gary, on the other hand, wasn't asking any questions. He was a planner by nature. "Last in Love" would be *their* song; the melody was slow enough for them to dance to on their fiftieth wedding anniversary. Harley would be there with his kids; maybe a couple more carrottops with their children—he made a mental note to look into additional children. He touched her hair and envisioned it streaked with gray, silver, copper, and gold. He'd be a rich man. He sighed contentedly.

Lu couldn't believe they were leaving all the fun so

early, the bar not closing for thirty minutes. Then she was totally bowled over when Gary bent low to kiss her on the cheek and thank her for coming.

For a split second Rose thought she saw tears welling in Lu's eyes. But then she laughed, warned them to set the parking brake if they weren't going straight home, blinked, and the tears were gone.

They walked the road back, a thin misty fog lending a romantic quality to the shadows and lights. Bill's was locked up tight, and the parking lot was empty except for Gary's truck. She hardly noticed that he opened the door for her again, but was acutely aware of the chilliness when he let go of her hand.

An atomic bomb couldn't have shattered the tension inside the cab. What could they say to each other during the twenty-minute ride home?

"I had a really good time."

"Me too."

"Lu's a character, isn't she?"

"She sure is."

What about kissing? Should he? Should she let him? Would it put her back on the defensive? What would it feel like? Anything close to what it felt like simply thinking about it? Would he expect more, or realize that she was merely curious? Good Lord, what about diet-soda breath?

Redgrove was asleep when they drove through, so missing Harley's bedroom light going out as they turned the corner would have been hard to manage.

Gary laughed softly in the dark beside her.

"He doesn't trust me yet either," he said idly.

The "yet" and "either" stung a bit.

"It's not that," she said, feeling a need to explain, wishing she had a blind faith in something, in anything inside her somewhere. "We're just not used to—"

"It should be that way," he interrupted. "It's okay. You don't have to trust everyone who comes along; you're smarter not to, especially if they're asking for as much as I want."

He deliberately parked the truck on the scarred concrete where the gas pumps once stood, under the burnt-out floodlight, blocking any view of them from the street.

"And what are you asking for?" she asked, her voice seeming too loud when he cut the soft purr of the engine.

He stared out the windshield for a second, then shifted his weight on the seat to face her.

"I want it all, Rose." "All" left her baffled. He'd have to get specific. "I want to be your lover, your pal, and your partner. Harley's male influence and Earl's . . . Earl's . . ."

"Speech therapist?"

He laughed. "Yeah. Earl's speech therapist. I want to be a part of your life. I want you in mine. I want a lot from you, Rose, and I'm more than willing to give you a lot in return. Including time."

"Time for what?"

"To get used to having me around."

Ah, why'd he have to ruin it? she wondered, semi-sick to her stomach, stiff in her chest. She couldn't remember becoming as fond of anyone as quickly as she had Gary. He was sharp and witty. Bright and dedicated. She enjoyed his company, felt good around him. Wasn't that enough? She didn't mind holding hands or dancing with him. And it was kind of fun to wonder what it would be like to kiss him; if his lips were as soft as they looked; if they'd send chills through her body the way his breath against her neck did; what his rough hands would do to her sensitive breasts, to the warm skin on her inner thighs. . . . But she could control herself. She *was* controlling herself. Why couldn't he?

The cab was suddenly a little too warm, and she didn't have any answers for him anyway. She decided to get out.

He came around the front of the truck and met her at the front door.

"I have to go home tomorrow." This didn't surprise her. She'd been waiting for him to tell her he had to leave. "On business. I'll be back on Wednesday." He paused as if he expected her to say something. "Can I see you?"

She shrugged. "I'll probably be here."

She made an intense study of the new marks on her white sneakers, pretending that she couldn't feel him watching her.

"Rose." She looked up. The softness in his voice brought her gaze to his. "I'll be back."

An unreasoning fear rose up within her. What if he didn't come back? What if he *was* like everyone else? What if there were a car accident? What if he picked up a homicidal hitchhiker? What if he had a weak heart? Lord, what if he were crushed under a few tons of trash?

Or simply disappeared? What then? What if she were doomed to wonder forever?

She flung her arms around his neck and locked his lips to hers.

Gary's shock was brief. He hardly wasted a second before looping an arm about her waist and threading his fingers into her soft and gloriously red hair. Where a pianist would shake his fingers loose of tension, he shuddered a sigh, nibbled her lower lip, then purged his restraint with a clean sweep of her honey sweet mouth. He wasn't a musician anyway.

Acting on her impulses was going to be the death of her. She could remember her mother telling her so as she stepped away slowly, feeling weak and debilitated—and as if she might like to die.

"It's . . . nice to have that over with, isn't it?" Gary said, laughing softly, teasing her gently, as if he could see the havoc in her soul.

She shook her head, disgraced.

"Ah, Rose," he said, folding his arms around her rigid form, unable to stop himself. "I'm glad you did it. One of us had to, and I would've looked like a masher."

"Now I look like one," she mumbled into his sweater.

"No. You can't," he said, stroking her hair. "Only men can be mashers; women are something else. I read that somewhere."

Awk! He was an impossible man, she decided again, stepping away. He had an answer for everything, and when he didn't he'd simply make something up.

"I should go in," she said. Already she was beginning to wish she'd paid closer attention to the kiss. All she could remember was how shockingly wonderful it had been, none of the specific details of it.

She opened the door and walked inside. It was always open, because the lock had rusted years after they lost the key to it.

"I'll see you on Wednesday." He paused. "Would you like to eat out again?"

"On a Wednesday?"

"It happens."

Of course it did. She worked Wednesdays till ten.

"I work that night."

"Okay. I'll come late and walk you home."

She was going to remind him that she worked across the street, but he knew that. He was teasing her. She smiled.

"Thank you for the nice time."

"You're welcome. And thank you."

She closed the door quietly, needing something ordinary to concentrate on. She climbed into the shadows of the stairwell, waiting for the sounds of his leaving, then turned and plopped down on the third step from the top, and buried her face in her hands.

"He's a garbageman. He's a garbageman," she began to chant, wishing he'd come back, hoping the yen in the pit of her stomach wouldn't last long. "He's a garbageman. . . ."

There was a soft rapping-on-glass sound at the door. He was back. He was holding the little potted rosemary plant; she could see it from her hiding place.

The soft rapping came again. She stood on trembling legs and went down the steps to the door.

"You forgot this," he said, holding the pot out to her. The tips of their fingers touched as she took it, and lightning shot up her arms and down her spine.

"Thank you," she said, making the mistake of looking at him, of meeting his gaze. Oh dear, did she look as eager to kiss again as he did? Did her attraction show as badly? Was her desire as raw? Her hopes as obvious?

Yep.

She watched as his face came closer and closer, mesmerized, shocked by the tenderness and affection in his expression, the longing and the need—for her. *For her.*

His lips brushed hers, returned to press lightly, sweetly. Something warm and devastating swept through her, made her tremble. She felt his hands at her shoulders as her weight sagged against the door frame for support. His lips became urgent, his mouth hot and demanding, taking what she had forgotten how to give. He blew gently on nearly cold embers of passion, nursing them carefully, skillfully back to life.

Heat rose up within her. In her heart she could hear the walls of the dam cracking and bursting apart. She felt the power and strength of her pent-up emotions as they came crashing through the barriers.

Gary pulled away, looking as numb and confused and overwhelmed as she felt. Her chest was heaving; she couldn't get enough air. Her hands were shaking.

Her knees wobbled, and she plastered herself to the doorjamb to keep from falling when he reached out to caress her cheek with the soft skin on the back of his fingers. She swallowed hard at the hunger in his eyes, and felt pain in her chest at the adoration.

"Good night, Rosemary," he murmured.

She nodded slightly, unable to speak, ravaged by so many emotions, she couldn't feel anything. She stood there like a cigar store indian . . . maybe more like a plant stand, she supposed, taking in the scent of rosemary, holding the pot close as she watched him drive away. She was frowning. She had the distinct feeling she was forgetting something.

SIX

Waiting for Wednesday wasn't wise. She knew this. But not thinking about it was like trying to put out the fires of hell with an empty bucket.

Making coffee at the diner, she wondered how he would arrive on Wednesday night. In some outrageous and ridiculous fashion, no doubt. In sparkling sequins, maybe, barely outstriding a cheering crowd of adoring fans to bend her back over his arm and kiss his seal of ownership upon her lips? Sigh. Or on a dazzling white horse, with trumpets blasting as he rides into town, sweeps her off her feet, and gallops away into the sunset? Sigh. Sigh. Or would he descend slowly from the sky in a brightly colored balloon, lift her into the basket, kiss her, and turn up the gas for their getaway? Sigh. Sigh. Sigh. Sigh.

"Allergies?"

"What?" She looked over her shoulder at Lu, who was counting out change in the cash register.

"You sound as if you're having trouble breathing. Are your allergies acting up?"

"I don't have allergies," she said, stepping down from the stool she'd used to reach the top of the coffeemaker.

"It's probably all the smoke and fumes from that torch you use. I'll bet it's harder on your lungs than cigarettes. You should have it checked out."

"I'm not sick." I'm an idiot, she added mentally. I'm interested in a man. A garbageman, no less. Another big deep sigh. She went off to clean the restrooms before they opened for breakfast. Her whole day was pretty much in the toilet anyway.

She tightened the vises holding the curved portion of a bed frame at a right angle to the wrought-iron candlestick she'd found at the All Bright dump the week before. Not that it looked like a candlestick anymore. She'd cut off the top and bent the four rods out a little, as if it were blooming.

What on earth could she say when she saw him again? She had less than twenty-four hours to come up with some calm, polite but firm—very firm—way of telling Gary she couldn't see him anymore.

"I like you," she said aloud to practice an uncompromising tone of voice. "I like you a lot. More than I thought I would . . . no, more than I thought I could." She paused. "Better," she muttered inside her mask, wanting every word to be perfect. Truthful and absolute, but not cutting. "But this isn't going to work out. I'm set in my ways. I'm used to doing things my way. There just isn't any room in my life for you."

"There's no room in anyone's life for 'em," Harley said from the doorway, startling her. It was a favorite game of his since childhood. "They're too big. I've been telling you that. Who's going to put something like that in their living room?" he asked, long-legging it across the concrete floor, assuming that she'd been talking to her sculptures. "They're okay. I mean, they're not a piece of sheet metal with four holes in it, not as lame as most of 'em in that book of yours. They're sort of interesting. Different. But they aren't beautiful, Mom. Not like the others." He wrapped a supportive arm around her shoulders and added, "You can talk to 'em all you want, but I don't think it's gonna help. They're not like flowers, you know."

"Those flowers out front are beautiful," she told Lu one morning. "When did you plant them?"

"They're perennial. They come up every year."

"They do?" She looked out the window at them. "Were they there last year?"

"Every year since I bought this place. Where have you been?"

Rose couldn't tell her.

She spent too much time Wednesday morning wondering what to wear. Generally she wore her red apron over jeans and some sort of shirt, with her worn-out sneakers. But for no reason she wanted to think about, that particular Wednesday she felt like wearing something a little different, a little nicer. . . . For no good reason.

Her room looked like Harley's by the time she decided to go with her newest blue jeans, a green plaid cotton oxford shirt, and her good white sneakers with the black smudges across the toes. She'd have to be careful not to get gravy or spaghetti sauce on them. You couldn't blast Lu's spaghetti sauce stains out with dynamite.

"New shoes?" Danny O'Brian asked when she entered the diner. It was three in the afternoon, and he was still out to lunch.

"No. They've got smudges. See?"

"Sure look new," he insisted.

"Well, they're newer than my old ones, but they're not brand new."

Lord above. You'd have thought she was wearing diamonds and pearls. Any minor deviation from the norm, and tongues started wagging. Next they'd start thinking she was dressed up for something special.

"That's a nice plaid with that red hair of yours," Emma Motley, Redgrove's postmistress, commented kindly.

"It's not new either. What is this sudden interest in my clothes? I wear shirts and sneakers every day, and you don't say anything about it. What's so special about today?" she asked, a bit testy. "I've had this shirt for six years. I just don't wear it often. . . ."

Her voice trailed off when she noticed that her attitude was drawing more attention than her clothes.

"You know," Lu said, poising a pencil at her lips thoughtfully. "I don't think I've seen you wear that particular shade of lipstick before. What's it called?"

She fought a sudden impulse to chew it all off.

"She don't usually wear lipstick, does she?" Emma asked, seeming confused. "Nor rouge neither, come to think of it."

"Who's this we're talking about now," Lucy Flannary asked, entering the diner. She walked up to her usual stool at the lunch counter and set her purse on the seat beside her, saying, "Martin is driving me crazy today. We ordered in some new summer cottons, and he's over there mixing and matching the colors with all the blues here and the reds there, and the oranges and the yellows, and 'Is this more red or more orange?' he asks me. 'Is this one more green or blue?' I rue the day that man retired. I swear he's going to drive me to drink. I'll have a cherry cola, Lu. Now, who doesn't wear rouge?"

"Rosie," Danny and Emma said together. Emma nodded, "Nor lipstick neither."

Lucy considered Rose for a moment, then said, "Well, sure she does. What's the matter with you? Not that she needs to with that fine redheaded complexion she's got, but she always looks really pretty on Sundays when she brings Harley to church and when she goes down to see that artsy fella in the city and for the church socials and . . . well, for most special events."

They all looked at Rose. She could almost hear the gears in their heads grinding and screaming, metal against metal, as they tried to recall exactly what it was that was so special about that particular Wednesday. It was deafening.

"It's lipstick, for crying out loud!" she exclaimed, her hands palm up in front of her. "A little powdered blush. That's all." She pointed an accusing finger at Lu. "She wears it all the time. And eye shadow too."

But you're not Lu was written all over their faces.

"It's nothing. A whim. Oh, you people are impossible. Think whatever you like," she said confidently, knowing that Gary wouldn't come until closing time and that her lipstick would be long gone by then. She took a clean red apron from the linen cupboard and snapped it smartly before tying it around her waist. Her arms akimbo, she addressed Lu in a businesslike fashion, "What's the dinner special?"

Strange. Fried chicken with potatoes and thick, sticky gravy, kernel corn, and biscuits seemed to appeal to almost everyone in town that night. Lucy left to close up the fabric shop and returned with Martin to have dinner at the diner. Danny O'Brian called his wife from the hardware store and said he'd treat her to a dinner out if she'd meet him at Lulu's about six-thirty. Some of the fishermen came straight from their boats at sundown, families in tow. Several lumberjacks, old buddies of Earl, moseyed in with their wives and children.

By eight Lu had called Harley and Earl on the phone and sent them after buckets of the Colonel's chicken in Arcata. And could they stop at Safeway for potato flakes and instant gravy? Maybe a few more cans of corn and those tubes of biscuits too? And be sure to come to the back door. . . .

Rose was too busy to be suspicious until she noticed that they were lingering over their desserts and she was pouring gallons of coffee by the cup. Why weren't they leaving? She looked at the clock. Nine-thirty. They closed at ten-thirty. Gary said he'd come late. If they didn't start leaving pretty soon, they'd all be there when he came and . . .

Oh no. Instant headache.

She heard Lu chuckling in the kitchen and looked up as she plopped a cherry atop a root beer float.

"What's so funny?" she asked, praying Gary wouldn't do anything stupid like . . . smile at her when he got there.

"I was just wondering if you were planning to wear lipstick again tomorrow. The special is liver and onions."

She gave her a torpid look.

"Why are they doing this to me?" she whispered miserably. "Don't they have televisions? Don't any of them collect stamps or go bowling or knit or have anything else more interesting to do than to watch me?"

"In a word, no," she said. The look on Rose's face tore at her heart, and she took mercy on her. "Look, honey, don't let it get to you. They love you."

"Right."

"They do. And you've been asking for this for . . . well, for at least the ten years I've known you."

"What are you talking about? Asking for what?"

She set the float on the counter and leaned into the window as far as she could. "I haven't done anything."

"My point exactly. Rosie, honey, you've been walking a very fine, very straight line for the past fifteen years. You've kept your nose too clean, your life too quiet. Too mistake-proof for too long. Gary's the first exciting thing that's happened to you since Harley was born. They just want to share it with you, is all."

"Is all?" She would have said more—something about the right to privacy and the unprincipled practices of small-town gossipmongers—but the bell over the front door jingled and she had a temporary heart attack.

Harley and Earl walked in, looking around the diner with great curiosity. Several people at the lunch counter moved down a space so they could take the last two seats side by side.

"Hey, Mom. What's happenin'?"

"Nothing. Is your homework done?"

"Yeah. What's goin' on here?"

"Nothing. What are you doing here? Why aren't you getting ready for bed? Earl, do you want an iced tea?" The old man gave her a quick nod.

"He was worried," Harley said, speaking of his grandfather. "Couldn't figure out why there were still so many people over here at this time of night. Thought you might need more chicken or somethin'."

"I don't know why everyone's still here, honey," she said, extra loud. "You'd think they were all watching for a circus to come through town."

Harley grinned, a Redgrover born and bred.

"Well, it's not coming," he shouted back at her. "The ringmaster called to say he couldn't make it tonight. He'll be here tomorrow."

The low moan of disappointment that rumbled through the diner set Rose's cheeks ablaze. And when people started reaching for their jackets and sweaters and pushing their sleepy children to stand and leave, tears of embarrassment gathered in her eyes. The words "stood up" drifted through the air once or twice, and she wished the linoleum floor would open up and swallow her.

The jingle of the bells over the door set off an angry alarm in her head.

"The special tomorrow night is liver and onions," she called to her neighbors as they left. "And if you stay for the show, you'll have to buy tickets!"

"Harley!" She yelled loud enough for him to hear her at the back of the garage where he'd been banging a basketball against the wall for the past two hours. She was holding a heavy piece of six-inch metal tubing above her head. "Har-ley. Come help me." The pounding on the wall stopped, but the throbbing in her head continued. "Hustle it."

She caught a movement to her left through the small window in her mask. "I broke my vise. See if you can find another, will you? And hurry, please, this is heavy." Tools clinked and clanked behind her, and her arms grew weaker by the second. "Hell's bells, just forget it," she snapped with instant regret. Earlier he'd likened her disposition to Godzilla on PCP, and it was extremely irritating every time she proved him right. "Come hold this and I'll find it."

The weight was released immediately, and she looked up to make sure he had a good hold, but the hands she saw weren't Harley's. She twisted her neck sharply, and painfully, to meet Gary's eyes through the window of her mask. Her heart jumped into her throat.

"Where'd you come from?"

"What?"

"Where'd you come from?"

His eyes twinkled in at her. "Heaven?"

She let go of the pipe, stepped around him, and pushed up her mask on the way to her work table.

"What are you doing here?" she asked.

"Nothing much. Until you started screaming, I was shootin' hoops with Harley. But then I came running in here to rescue you."

That wasn't what she meant, but she knew he knew that. Why couldn't he just answer her questions? Couldn't he simply start explaining the whys and the wherefores without her having to ask specifically where he was and why he hadn't come the night before? She kept her back to him, torn between an everlasting gratitude that he hadn't shown up at the diner, and eternal loathing for having stood her up in front of nearly everyone she knew. She vacillated between an unmistakable joy and excitement at seeing him again, and the dull ache of common sense in her head that was advising her to run for her life.

Okay. She was a little confused.

She tossed heavy tools back and forth on the table, then glanced over her shoulder at him. "How long have you been here?"

"A couple hours, I think. You were working, so the kid offered me the opportunity to work up a good sweat." He didn't look sweaty. He looked big and healthy and handsome. "He's got one hell of a slam dunk. He's good."

"He should be. I've spent a small fortune on basketballs for him to bang against that wall over the last nine or ten years. It's a wonder they haven't come all the way through yet," she said, though she had never really begrudged Harley his basketballs. Last season he played on the varsity team as a high school freshman, and no mother could have been prouder than Rose Wickum.

"Not to change the subject," he said mildly. "But I hear you missed me last night."

"What?" Her voice broke and squeaked as she spun around to face him. Would this nightmare never end?

He chuckled, adjusting his hands on the pipe so he could turn and see her better. "Would you mind taking your hood off? All I can see is your eyes. You look like an owl in there."

"Yes, I would mind." Her face was on fire. "I'm working."

"Is that what you're looking for there?" he asked, holding the pipe with one hand and waving a finger of the other at the table.

"Don't drop that now," she said, scanning for the spare vise in a hurry. "I don't have a solid weld on it yet." She found it. "And I didn't miss you. I was glad you didn't show up. Did Harley tell you what happened?"

He bowed his body to let her in front of him, closer to the joint she was working on, and watched her long, thin fingers deftly fit and fasten the clamp. He liked her hands. They were graceful, strong, and sure. They were talented hands.

"He said the whole town missed me last night. I guess I assumed that meant you did too."

"That's your problem," she said, grunting as she tightened the clamp with all her strength. "You assume a lot."

"Humph. I wasn't aware that I had a problem. Another false assumption, I assume."

The digging humor in his voice told her that if he thought he could get away with it, he'd put his fingers to her ribs and tickle a smile to her lips.

She took a deep breath.

"At least this way we can talk in private," she said, turning to face him. "You can let go now."

He did, and he let his arms fall down behind her, skillfully catching her in his embrace.

"Are we going to talk serious?" he asked, peering through the opening in the mask at her.

"Yes," she said, acting indifferent to his nearness while her pulse raced. Fighting him would only make him think she cared, or was a little too excited, or that she enjoyed being there too much. Indifference wouldn't tell him anything. "Very serious. This has got to stop. I can't—"

"I can't talk serious to a woman wearing a welding

mask. I'm sorry. All I can think of is Darth Vader." She closed her eyes and prayed for patience. Then she reached up and removed the hood. "Ah, much better," he said, almost reverently, his gaze brushing over her red hair and clear pale skin, flushed with heat. "So beautiful."

Then he was kissing her. It was a second or two before she realized where the sudden burst of bliss was coming from. With one gloved hand full of welding hood and the other pushing feebly against his chest—and two more hands reaching out from somewhere deep inside her to pull him close and hold him near!—something snapped in the middle, and she came untied in his arms. She dropped the mask as if she were a beaten prizefighter, throwing in the towel.

After all, toe-curling kisses were not meant to be rejected. Really. It was unnatural. Instinctively one gave into the tingles and chills shooting through one's body and the warm coil of need twisting low in one's abdomen. Intuitively one sought the source of the pleasure and allowed an inborn greed—found in all of us—to seek out more of the same delight. Demand it even. And when one's mind was reeling beyond discriminate thought and the sensations began to ebb away, leaving one weak and breathless, it was the most natural thing in the world to rest one's head on a broad shoulder and wonder at the sound of another heart beating as fast as one's own. The most natural thing in the world. Truly. Look it up.

Gary held her in his arms, rocking her gently, sensing the chaos inside her. As a matter of fact, it didn't make much sense to him either. Of the, let's guesstimate and say, one hundred women he'd taken an interest in over the past twenty years, he'd wanted to love them all. He'd tried really hard with a couple of them, and had married one once, believing that respect and friendship were as good as it was ever going to get. Then one bright sunny morning he had spied Rose atop a pile of trash, and falling in love had been as easy as crushing an empty cereal box. Did that make sense?

Now his poor Rose was struggling. Not with falling in love, that was happening on its own. He could see it in her eyes and feel it deep in his bones. Nothing in his life felt more genuine or critical than loving Rose. But Rose simply didn't, or couldn't, understand it.

"Maybe you shouldn't fight it so hard," he murmured, her hair tickling his lips. He rested his chin on the top of her head. "Maybe . . . maybe just trying to enjoy it will make it less scary. Love's not always a bad thing, you know." He paused. "I can't tell you it doesn't hurt, you know it does. I can't promise I won't hurt you, because I might. But I can tell you that you'll never know for sure unless you come out on this limb with me."

She looked up, as if she had something important to tell him, but then she bowed her head and stepped away.

"I've been out on that limb before. It's not very strong," she said, removing her thick apron and tossing it onto the work table with her gloves.

"No," he said. "You've never been out on this particular limb. You might have tried a couple that were weak, that failed you. But every chance you take is a different limb. It might look the same, but you don't know what it's made of; you don't know how strong it is until you try it."

She had the sudden image of her Tree of Chances looking something like a stock of bamboo in tall grass.

But something in his words rang true in some deep dark pocket of hope she'd hidden away years earlier. He wasn't like anyone she'd ever known before. For one thing, his persistence was remarkable. She knew her cold shoulder had frostbitten a few men's fingers over the years. He seemed impervious to it. In fact, it amused him—which was something else about him she liked. He made her laugh and feel young. She hadn't felt so young since . . . since she was young. Over the past week she'd taken to daydreaming and fussing in front of the mirror, and adding three caps of bubble bath to the water instead of her usual, practical one capful. He'd reintroduced her to anticipation, excitement, sexual desire, and whistling before breakfast. He was almost enough to make her want to shimmy to the top of her bamboo shoot and risk the wind trying to blow her off.

"Rose?" She turned to look at him. It might have been her imagination, but he looked to be standing a little taller, a little straighter than his usual loose and casual stance. The word "determined" came to mind. "You might have noticed that I have ways of getting what I want. My mother says I'm like a junkyard dog with a new bone when my mind is set on something. My brothers say, well, I won't tell you what they say.

You might have a fair idea already." His smile was borderline sheepish. "I operate my life by dancing around and talking fast until people's minds are spinning. Then, while they're staggering around, dizzy and out of focus, I do what I want. I build incinerators and get environmental protection laws passed through the state legislature and rezone properties for landfill and . . . well, pretty much anything else I want to do. The thing is, I don't want to bully you into anything you're dead set against. But I'm not going to make it easy for you to get rid of me either. I don't give up without a fight."

If he had a gauntlet—or even a dirty old work glove—he might have thrown it at her feet. But Rose wouldn't have picked it up. She didn't need to. She was ready to surrender.

She was aware of a crushing loneliness within her. A singleness that made her feel small and exposed and defenseless. It was a feeling she'd first experienced when her mother had died. A spectator sensation, as if she were an all-star player watching the game from the sidelines. And here was the neighborhood boy asking the new kid on the block if she wanted to play. Here was a welcoming hand, waving her off the bench and into the circle of the living, the feeling, the loved.

"We're having fish for dinner," she said, walking past him toward the stairs.

"What kind?" he asked, watching her, sensing that he'd won the battle, very aware that the war was far from over.

"Red snapper."

"With capers?"

"Nope. Secret family sauce."

"What's for dessert?" he asked, following her up the stairs.

"Something sweet."

SEVEN

As wars went, theirs was like trying to get a tan by candlelight. It simply wasn't happening.

"Go ahead. Ask him," Lucy said, flicking her fingers first at Rose, then in Gary's direction. He'd taken to hanging around the diner for two-hour lunches, sometimes staying on to have dinner. Within a matter of days, he'd been assigned his own swivel chair at the lunch counter and weaseled himself into a prominent position in Redgrove society. "Can't hurt to ask," she insisted.

"Ask me what?" he said, returning to his seat after a lengthy long-distance call from his office in San Francisco. There wasn't a speck of dust on the old pay phone in the corner these days. Lu and Rose had all but forgotten it was there until Gary started taking calls on it, explaining that three quarters of what he did was done by telephone and one phone was as good as the next. When someone finally asked why he didn't have one of them newfangled cellular phones, he said he'd had four and lost them all.

"Lucy and Martin comanage the Rangers, and they want to know if you'll try out," Rose said, picking up a set of salt and pepper shakers in one hand and pushing the black metal napkin holder and sugar to one side so she could wipe the counter underneath them with the other.

"Do I have to ride a horse?" he asked.

"It's baseball," she said, working her way down to him. "The Redgrove Rangers. We've come in second place to the Eureka Eagles two years in a row now. This year we're taking them to the cleaners."

"You play baseball?" he asked her, his eyes round with wonder. She also read murder mysteries—his favorite; loved butternut ice cream—his favorite. She thought the dream sequence on *Dallas* was a cop-out; that almost any anonymous, basically honest, apolitical Joe Schmoe with a high school education could balance the national deficit within twenty-four months; that Anita Hill got a raw deal—and he did too. She preferred to get her world news from newspapers and not television; she ate fruit chews at the movies instead of popcorn; *and* she played baseball?

"This girl lives for baseball," Lu said, pushing through the kitchen door, carrying a rack of clean glasses. "She cried for a week when Harley dropped out of Little League and took up basketball."

"Too much pressure," Emma Motley said, straightening the collar of her postal uniform. "He was smart to see that he couldn't play as good as his mother."

"He was eight years old," Rose said in Harley's defense. After so many years she still felt a little guilty for taking him to her games while he was struggling to develop his own skills. "Harley's good at whatever he wants to be good at, which is basketball . . . and video games . . . and anything else that doesn't have a thing to do with his education."

The ten-man lunch rush chuckled.

"So?" Lucy asked, leaning forward to look down the counter at Gary. "Do you like baseball or don't you?"

"Did Matty Mathewson pitch three shutouts in the 1905 World Series? Did Babe Ruth ever clout a hundred and twenty-five homers in an hour? Did Ty Cobb hit over four thousand in the major leagues? Was he the best base stealer ever? Was Willie Keeler—"

"We practice on Mondays and play on Fridays," Lucy broke in. "Six o'clock sharp both nights."

"I won't play unless I can have first base or shortstop," he said, as if he were negotiating a major league contract.

"I'm first base," Rose told him, all but putting up her dukes to defend her position.

"You'll have to try out for shortstop against Joe Spencer," Lucy said. "We don't play favorites."

"Joe Spencer? The guy who owns Mike's Auto Parts? He's only got one leg," he said, trying to get a clear picture of the competition.

"Hell of a mechanic," Danny said, wiping his fingers and mouth free of french-fry salt and ketchup with a paper napkin. "But he's a little slow behind the pitcher. Better in the outfield."

And so it was that the King of Trash became a Redgrove Ranger, her teammate, committed for the baseball season.

It wasn't a great deal of time, but it was more than she'd let herself hope for. She had to keep reminding herself that as wonderful as it was to have him around—to look forward to seeing him each day, to laugh with him, to talk and hold hands and share a sunset with him, to feel his lips on hers and to experience emotions with such intensity that it frightened her, to be so incredibly happy—it wasn't going to last forever. She was determined to enjoy Gary minute by minute for as long as she could.

You see, Rosemary Wickum knew the truth about herself. She was a single. She had no match, no mate, no soul companion. It wasn't the life she would have chosen, but it was the life she got, and she'd accepted the fact that no one would stay in her life forever. Especially if she loved them.

Nobody stayed. Not her mother. Not her father. Not Harley's father. She'd grown up alone. Raised her child alone. It seemed logical and fitting that she grow old alone.

That was probably why she loved Earl so much, even if he was an old poop. And why she cherished every battle, every joke, every hug she shared with Harley. The time they were giving her to love them was a gift, and when they were gone all she would have were the memories.

Gary slipped neatly into that niche as well. She was falling hard and deeply in love with him, but he wouldn't stay. Why would he? Earl stayed because she was living in his house and he couldn't get away from her. She was also a convenience. Harley stayed because she was his mother and for a while yet he needed her. But she hadn't been enough to keep her father from drinking himself to death, hadn't been a good enough reason for her mother to live, hadn't had whatever it would have taken to get Harley's father to marry her. . . . Why would Gary stay?

She was only average height with unruly red hair, and she probably wasn't as strong as Earl said. She had no college education, lived in a gas station, worked in a diner, and dreamed of turning scrap metal into something beautiful. It wasn't a bad life overall. However, upon close scrutiny there wasn't much in her life that would induce a man, particularly one as energetic as Gary, to stick around.

No, her time with Gary was a gift. Maybe something she'd earned after so many years of being alone. An oasis in her journey across life's desert. Whatever. She wasn't going to meddle with it or question it or measure how long it was. It was enough, more than enough, more than she'd expected to be in love again, to feel silly and happy and young. It was a gift.

It wasn't long before the announced sightings of Rose and Gary walking hand in hand on the beach were as old and predictable as rain in the weather forecast. The townspeople encouraged the two of them to play catch in the street—they were both a little out of shape after the winter. They smiled when they saw Gary and Harley talking and shadowboxing as they walked to the Safeway on some errand for Rose.

Of course, it was Gladys Ford's job to keep an eye on the comings and goings of Gary's pickup truck. She lived in the small upstairs apartment over her daughter's shop. Betty's Boutique, Hair and Nails, Open Tuesday thru Saturday, 8 to 4:30.

"Lands alive, they were doin' some heavy-duty window steamin' in the truck last night," Gladys told Betty first thing when she came up the stairs to check on her mother that morning. "He still ain't staying though. Can't figure it out. Nice, good-lookin', healthy boy like that. . . . Don't know what little Rosie's thinkin', leadin' him on. Lord knows she wasn't playin' hard to get when she got young Harley-boy. Sat in the truck awhile after she went in last night. Must be painin' him some to leave her every night."

"Mama," Betty said, turning red faced.

"Aw, there ya go, Miss Priss. A man's got feelin's, too, ya know. 'Member, I told ya that's how I got my first clothes-washin' machine from your daddy. Didn't touch him for a whole two weeks and presto! There it was all bright and shiny and new come Saturday mornin'." She laughed and slapped the arm of her wheelchair with her hand a couple of times.

"I don't think Rose needs a new washer, Mama. I think she's being careful this time. Do you want your hair washed this morning?"

"Careful? Careful of what?"

"Of her feelings," the divorced mother of two said,

preparing to wash her mother's hair. "Of making another mistake."

"Hell's afire," Gladys muttered. "The whole town can see they're made for each other. Rosie and her garbageman. Be a shame if she let him get away. Maybe I should have a talk with her."

"Mama, don't you dare start yelling out your window at her again. She'll make up her own mind."

"Well, she better hurry up about it. Use the other stuff that doesn't smell like dandelions, honey girl. That boy's goin' to pop wide open if he doesn't get some lovin' soon."

"A picnic?"

"Yeah. A picnic. With a blanket and food and ants. Flies and bees, too, maybe. Out in the middle of nowhere. No phones. No traffic. No binoculars. No crazy old ladies hanging out their windows screaming 'Go for it' at us. We need to get away."

"You're just now coming to this conclusion?" she asked, yawning. She stretched her naked body long and tight under the bedsheet that covered them. She felt his hand move down her taut abdomen to her thighs and up again, his palm flat in the valley between her breasts. She covered his hand with hers, moved it slightly to the left, above her heart, so he could feel the way he made it race. "I can see college did you a lot of good."

"At least now I know how my biology experiments felt," he mumbled into the pillow beside her ear, his thumb strumming her nipple, slow and lazy. "Who's the guy who runs the convenience store again? I keep forgetting his name."

"Bobby Roberts?"

"Mmm. I stopped to get a newspaper yesterday, and he tried to sell me a *Playboy.*" Her laugh came out like a snort through her nose. "Can you believe that? He came right out and told me that sometimes he uses them to get his motor started. Said it was nothing I should be ashamed of. . . . Stop laughing. This is getting to be embarrassing. I'm serious. Stop it."

Of course, the more serious he got, the harder she giggled. His scowl brought tears to her eyes, and when he turned his back on her, she rolled over and screamed helplessly into the pillow.

Actually she was very proud of her partner in crime. For weeks now they'd been having hot, wild, passionate sex and making sweet, tender love under the noses of everyone in Redgrove, and no one knew it but them. A real live secret. No small accomplishment.

He would come to her in the morning or in the early afternoon when Harley was at school and Earl, with his keen and mute perception, had disappeared for the day. He'd attack her like a hungry beast or torture her long and sweet before he took her, and then they'd dress and walk on the beach or shower together and swing in the hammock in the backyard, in full view of her neighbors.

Only God knew what the gossips thought the two of them were doing every day for the hour or two they were closed up in the garage together. She suspected that they all thought sex was strictly a nocturnal activity.

More's the pity for them, she thought, flipping onto her back with her hands behind her head.

From his deep regular respirations she could tell that Gary had dozed off in his snit. She smiled. She wished she had his patience. His wisdom too.

Though maybe he wasn't as wise as much as he had good instincts about people. Like a con man. He always knew the right thing to say to people. He knew when to touch them and when to back off. For certain, he could play her like a fiddle at a barn dance, she thought, recalling their first time together. . . .

He'd invited her to take an afternoon drive with him and she'd accepted. It was a bright sunny morning, but as they drove the highway south toward Eureka, the wind picked up and dark clouds rolled in from the west. They turned off the asphalt before they got there, onto the unpaved road through Myrtletowne and Freshwater. And lo and behold, they weren't too far from where he was living! Big surprise. Would she like to see the place?

They were dancing around the fire like a couple of cowardly fire walkers, performing all the right rituals and intoning all the ancient chants, slow and meticulous, knowing all the while that eventually, inevitably, they were going to have to step on those hot coals.

She couldn't believe how nervous she was, walking up the wide set of steps to the front porch of the old farmhouse. It wasn't as if she hadn't done it before, or wasn't expecting it or didn't want to have sex with him.

Frankly, she was on the verge of losing what little sanity she had left to an undeniable craving that needed to be satisfied soon.

She stuffed her trembling hands into the bend of each elbow, crossing her arms in front of her, and gave serious consideration to the view.

"It's pretty out here," she said, listening to the overgrown grass in the fields surrounding the house, rustling in the wind. "I can still smell the ocean."

"It's in the wind," he said, standing behind her. Too close behind her. She couldn't actually feel him, but he was close enough to invade that invisible personal space around her body and send her senses into a supersensitive red alert. "It's almost thirty miles straight off that way," he said, pointing west. "At night I think I can hear it sometimes. The old man I bought it from said his mother picked this site special. He said his father was a fisherman and his mother used to have nightmares about him dying at sea. She'd go to the window a thousand times a day to look out at the sea for him, waiting for him to come home every night. For years she did this. Then one winter she decided she couldn't live beside the ocean anymore. She wanted to move inland. She pestered her husband and pestered him, the way women do . . ." He chuckled when Rose glowered over her shoulder at him. ". . . until finally he gave in, on one condition."

"There's always a condition."

"She could build her new house anywhere she wanted, so long as he could still smell the ocean from the front porch." He turned to rest against the porch railing, facing her. "So, she started sniffing on the beach—"

"Oh, stop," she broke in, seeing that it was another of his elaborate and very stupid jokes. "I'm not going to believe another word you say."

He tried to look hurt.

"I swear, the old man told me his mother started sniffing the air on the beach just north of Humboldt Bay and started walking east. She had the front door built exactly one foot from the last place she could smell the ocean."

"I don't believe you," she said, refusing to laugh, though she knew her lips were twitching.

"Go stand over by the door and sniff," he said in earnest.

"No."

"Why not?"

"Because if I go over there and start sniffing around, you'll have some asinine punch line, and I'll look like an idiot again. No thank you."

"I swear I'm telling the truth."

"Swear all you want."

"I don't lie, Rose."

"Gary," she said, placing her palms on his chest. "If I go over there and sniff and get a nose full of ocean, and you—"

"I won't. Trust me."

"Trust you?"

"Trust me," he said.

Even as she took the first step backward, she felt sure she'd fall through a rotten spot in the porch or walk smack into the brunt of this week's ha-ha. Still, there was something in his eyes and in the set of his firm jaw that insisted that she trust him this time. It was important to him that she could trust him, blindly.

Her hands behind her, feeling the way, she backed up slowly, her eyes never wavering from his. She felt the screen door with her fingertips and pressed her back to the weathered siding. He was waiting for her to inhale, and she was putting it off, wondering how disappointed she'd be if it was a joke after all.

Finally she drew in a lungful of air through her nose. She did it again, her olfactory nerve finely honed to kelp and salt. Nothing. She could smell the grass and the distinctive scent of moist forest soil, but no ocean. Her gaze met his across the porch with instant recognition. She'd been duped. Tricked into trusting him, despite her misgivings . . . his objective all along.

She lowered her eyes to the planking on the porch, confused and frightened. Had she always been so easy to manipulate? Or did he have some mystic power over her? She'd sensed he was up to something; why hadn't she listened to her instincts? What if the stakes had been higher? What if next time . . .

He crossed the porch to her, knuckling her chin to tip her face up to his.

"Was that so terrible?" he asked, his voice light enough to be carried on the tail of an ocean breeze. "Was it so hard to trust me?"

"It was too easy," she said.

His smile was small but pleased, touched even.

"I don't lie, Rose. And I don't want to hurt you," he

said. His words were so plain and direct, they reminded her of that part of the Declaration that goes 'We hold these truths to be self-evident. . . .' And they were. She could see it in his eyes, feel it in the marrow of her bones.

"I know," she said.

His stroke of appreciation for her faith came as a tender, loving cupping of her cheek in the palm of his hand. She pressed against it. Her heart felt safe there. In the gentle palm of his hand.

"Would you like to see the inside of the house?" he asked, though they both knew that wasn't really what he was asking. If she chose to go in with him, they'd end up in bed. It was understood. Also accepted was her choice to decline.

"Yes. I'd love to."

He unlocked the door, and she followed him inside.

"Wow. You weren't kidding when you said it was a bed and a roof," she said, her voice echoing through the empty old farmhouse. She could smell old dust covered with a hint of lemon.

"This is the living room," he said, leading her around the first floor from one empty room to the next —still part of the fire-walker ceremony, she supposed.

All in all, it wasn't a bad house, she decided, letting her mind sneak away from the thoughts of what awaited them on the next floor. There were big windows in every room, showing the mountains to the east and rolling fields in all the other directions. For an empty house, it wasn't at all gloomy. The hardier rays of sunshine still pushing through the clouds, filled the recently wallpapered rooms and reflected off the shiny hardwood floors. And despite the fact that she could smell it, there wasn't any dust anywhere. Not the windowsills, the barren built-in bookshelves, or the floors.

The answer to that came soon enough—in the kitchen, where they found half a sinkful of cold soapy water and a broom resting over a pile of lint and dirt.

"Aw, damn," Gary muttered, flicking the stopper from the sink to let it drain while he searched for the dustpan. "I did a little cleaning this morning," he said, surprising her with his sudden fluster. He found the pan and quickly swept up the dust. "I wanted it to look nice. I mean, well, it's not a real home or anything, but I didn't want it to look like a . . . a . . ."

"A what?"

"A cheap motel," he said, making the words sound like an admission of guilt. They tore at Rose's heart. Who but Gary would have worried about such a thing? He always went out of his way to make everything they did together seem like something special.

She smiled. "I love these big old kitchens," she said, returning to the rite to ease his discomfort, though it did little for hers. She was growing weary of the dance and was eager to get to the main event.

"The old man said he spent the greater part of his life sitting at a big old maple drop-leaf table that sat over there," he said, nodding with his head. "His mother purposely put the kitchen at the back of the house so she wouldn't have to spend her days watching the road out front."

"How *did* her husband die?" She turned to move on to the next room. "Old age, I hope."

"He said that a year after they finished this house, to the day, his father died in a boating accident at sea."

She turned abruptly to see if he was pulling her leg again, and he caught her in his arms.

"Is that true?" she asked, overwhelmed by the awareness of his hands on her upper arms, of his mouth only inches away, of the quickening in his eyes.

"Would I lie to you?" She had the suspicion that if a prank were involved, he wouldn't hesitate. But then again, he'd just told her he wouldn't lie to her. When he could see that she was beginning to believe the story, he smiled. "It's hard to find a house with a story these days. That's one of the reasons I bought this one."

"One of the reasons?" she asked, turning to walk on, thinking it best not to stand too close to him for too long or they'd never make it to the second floor. "Are you planning to live here someday?"

"No. I needed a tax write-off." Whimsical, yet practical. A good definition of a Gary Albright, she thought. "See here," he said, taking two stairs at a time twice and bending low to point out a piece of wainscoting. "The old guy's name was Gabriel Peters." Deep in the woodwork, under a clean coat of white paint, were carved the initials GP. "There's ten of them. Every other step. One for each kid. He said his mother used to make them sit on their stair when they were in trouble." He moved up several more steps. "This poor guy's name was Pauly. Seems his brothers and sisters had a grand time with his initials. This one was Mary. MP. They called her Copper for fun. Like cops. Policemen?" he said when Rose didn't seem to understand.

"I got it," she said, still looking at him oddly. "I can't believe you remember all this stuff. All the names."

He grinned. "I told you. I like a good story. And why buy a house with a story if you can't remember it?"

"You like people, too, don't you?"

"I do," he said, walking up a few more stairs to the top. "I'm not too crazy about the way they handle their garbage, but for the most part I think they're pretty interesting." He waved an arm around in a vague gesture. "There are four bedrooms up here and two more on the third floor under the attic. I figure two kids to a room, the older boys upstairs, the girls and younger children down here . . . and the master bedroom," he said, stepping over to the first door on the right and pushing it open.

He moved to one side to let her enter. There was a big oak bed on the far wall with thick round bedposts at each corner, covered with a thick quilt with a blue and gold geometric pattern. There was a nightstand and a chest of drawers of the same wood and design. A lamp. No curtains. And the closet door was closed. It could have been a motel room. Until she spied a dog-eared copy of *The Firm* on the bedside table. It was his.

"You're pretty tidy for a man," she said, feeling she'd understated an anal-compulsive need for sterility. There were no pictures on the walls, no dirty socks, no crumpled newspapers, no aftershave on top of the dresser. Nothing but the book on the nightstand to show that someone lived there. It was still more the Peterses' house than Gary's.

"Bad habit," he said, watching her test the firmness of the bed's mattress. "Overcompensation for being the kid of a garbageman, I guess. Actually both my houses are like this," he added, walking slowly to the bed. "Houses, not homes. But all I do is sleep in them, and rarely at that."

What he meant to say was that he commuted so often between houses and hotel rooms in San Francisco and Sacramento, that he didn't often spend more than a week or two in a row in the same bed. But what Rose heard was that he rarely slept in his own bed, which meant he generally slept in someone else's. Most likely a woman's.

He sat down on the bed beside her, wishing he had a more intimate place to take her.

She stood up.

"I think we should talk," she said.

"Okay." He slipped a hand under each leg, trapping them as if he couldn't trust them.

She turned her back to him, walking slowly toward the closet as she spoke.

"You may have noticed that I'm not a young girl anymore," she said, her mouth as dry as her palms were clammy.

"Yes. I have."

"I mean, I'm not old, but I'm not young either."

"That would make you about . . . just right, then. Right?"

The smile she gave him over her shoulder was weak.

"The thing is," she said, opening the closet door with an irrational hope that he'd stuffed it full of smelly dirty clothes, banana peels, and porno magazines to make him seem much less perfect and polished. There were two dark suits, four dress shirts, about ten or twelve flannel shirts, and three pairs of casual slacks, all hung neatly on hangers. A cardboard box sat on the top shelf. Work boots, an extra pair of sneakers, and dress shoes were on the floor. She sighed dismally and closed the door.

"The thing is," she started again, facing him. "I don't have a lot of experience at this. I'm not a virgin, certainly. Not with Harley. But single mothers don't have the time to be as promiscuous as some people think, or used to think, maybe still think sometimes. I know I don't, haven't had the time, that is."

The look on her face made him want to burst into laughter, but it was far too serious for him even to attempt a smile.

"I hope you don't want me to say I'm sorry about that?"

"No, no. I don't want you to say anything about it." She really didn't. "I just . . . wanted you to know."

He nodded, properly advised of the situation. When he made no comment, she felt compelled to go on.

She laughed. "I don't even know where to begin." She laughed again, a little higher and a lot more nervous. "I think I've forgotten."

Again he swallowed the urge to laugh. Instead he pressed his lips together and gave a solemn nod as he got to his feet.

"I hear it's like riding a bike," he said, struggling to remain serious, tempted to rip her clothes off and give her a quick refresher course. "Once you've done it, you never really forget how." He shoved his hands deep into his pockets to appear less of a threat to her. "And lucky for us, it's been on my mind lately. Quite a bit. I think I have a vague recollection of how it works," he said, standing mere inches away from her, his hands turning to fists in his pockets as he looked into her clear and most wonderfully trusting green eyes. "If you want me to, I think I can guide you through it this first time."

He might have missed the slight nod of her head if he hadn't been so anxious for it. And he was. The fantasies he'd had as he'd watched her from afar, the dreams he'd had since they met, the reality of her touch and the taste of her mouth, were all taking a toll on his good but all-too-human nature. Frankly, he couldn't remember the last time he'd felt a need for a particular woman as deeply or intensely as he felt it for Rose.

"Take your shoes off," he said, his voice so unmanageably abrupt and gruff that it startled her. She did a quick toe-to-heel step with her shoes as he quickly tried to cover the sudden panic churning his guts. "If I'm not mistaken, we do this without clothes."

Now, let's face it, Gary was no stranger to the female form. It was his experience that women came rigged with the same basic equipment, differing only in size and color. He couldn't imagine finding anything new or unusual on Rose, so . . . why were his fingers numb? Stiff. Awkward with the buttons and holes down the front of her cotton shirt.

She moved suddenly, and he went rigid. Slow and tentative, her hands moved to the front of his shirt. She lowered her eyes from his to focus on her task. He bent his head to watch. She was trembling.

They were both giving serious consideration to clawing at and tearing away the minor inconveniences between them, but there was something profoundly physical, private, carnal, and downright exciting about unveiling each other for the first time.

He held his breath as he pealed her blouse from her shoulders, her white lacy bra looking delicate and feminine against the excited flush of her pale breasts. Her hands were cool to his overheated skin, her touch weightless and exploratory. His nipples grew hard when her palms passed over them. She could hear her heart pounding in her ears with his feather-light fingers between her breasts as he slipped the hook of her bra. Her skin prickled with gooseflesh, inside and out, when he brushed the bra away with the backs of his hands, cupping the soft, sensitive mounds in his palms.

Thunder rumbled in the distance . . . or just outside the window, it was hard to tell.

She lifted her face to his and felt a shiver of anticipation quiver through her when their eyes met. Powerful, passionate, possessive. Boldly she pressed her breasts against his palms, easing the ache and stirring the fire. She watched the hungry beast in his eyes target his prey. Keen. Confident. Lethal.

"A kiss about now could be interesting," he said, his tour-guide voice tight with need, his face already moving toward hers.

"To take the edge off?" She wondered aloud.

His devastating grin of comprehension and appreciation wasn't comforting.

"I don't think so," he said, his lips closing over hers.

His tongue slipped effortlessly into her mouth to taste and tease. Something close to pure delight washed through her as she did the same. Her mind reeled. His tense muscles turned to steal beneath her fingertips. A familiar medium. A material she knew she could control and manipulate, something she had power over.

Her artful hands went to work. Kneading. Stoking. Stressing. Establishing her authority. She went breathless when his arms snapped closed around her, crushing her to him. He was liquid molten ore, and he set her ablaze.

Lightning split the sky. Thunder rattled the windows.

It was a shock to discover that her powers were limited, humbling and thrilling at once. She was consumed by the basic elements of the material she was working with. Gary. The man. His texture. His taste. The sound of sweet misery low in his throat. The power in his strength. The purpose in his touch.

He made quick work of the rest of her clothes, his hands sure and masterful.

He tinkered with her. Rubbed her senses raw. Forged a sizzling pit of need within her. Molded her to him. Fashioned an unbreakable bond between them.

When she could no longer decipher the seam between them, where she stopped and he began, he took her, blending their souls into something new. Something never before known to man. As one, they were a mega-strength alloy. They were a composite of the best of them both. A perfect mixture. Created by God, conceived in the mind of Fate, manufactured by human need and ingenuity.

Rain pelted the windows and the thunder rolled into the distance as they lay spent in each other's arms. The hammering of his heart beneath her hand softened and slowed to a steady rhythm. His skin cooled, and he wrapped himself about her to keep them both warm. She began to cry.

"Rose? Aw, Rosie. Did I hurt you?"

"No, no. Not at all. No. I . . . remember," she said, and he chuckled. It was as if she were finishing their earlier dialogue. She reached up to draw his head back to her breast. She touched his dark hair, his whisker-rough cheek. "But I didn't know . . . I never knew . . . I never dreamed it could be like this."

He smiled and closed his eyes.

"That makes two of us," he said, tightening his arms around her, planning to hold on forever.

They didn't speak, but the room was far from silent. They sighed their contentment. Their love grew. Their doubts withered to dust. Happiness hummed in every corner. And hope built a solid foundation around them.

"Does everyone have to know about this?" she asked softly, a recurring thought creasing her brow.

"You mean, was I planning to put it in the newspaper? Gary Gets Lucky, see page one."

She laughed. "No. I mean, does everyone in Redgrove have to know we did this?"

He tipped his head back to look at her.

"You're embarrassed?"

"No. But . . ."

"What?"

"It was special." She closed her eyes. Now she *was* embarrassed.

"Tell me, Rose."

"I know you do this sort of thing all the time, so it's not a big deal for you. But it is to me."

"I beg your pardon?" He came up on one elbow. "I hope you're not trying to tell me it wasn't something special for me too. I've had sex before, but I've never done it with a woman I loved. I feel as if I've been wasting my time all these years."

She smiled. "I know. I mean, me too. I feel as if I've missed out on so much. I hate you for not coming around sooner."

"Then what are you worried about?"

She sighed, searching for words.

"This is mine. Ours. It's too wonderful, too new to be public knowledge. I want to keep it close. Keep it a secret. Just between the two of us. I don't want to have to see the looks or answer the questions or endure the jokes. Not yet. Not now."

Leaving one arm around her, he rolled onto his back and flung the other out straight.

"I want to dance a jig. I want to scream it from the rooftops. Rose, I've never felt like this before."

"Me either."

He turned his head in her direction. No price was too high for the warm glow that made her emerald eyes sparkle like gems. Her tender smile was a favor he would die for. Nothing in his world meant more to him, which was probably why he could sense the wariness in her. Not fear or shame, but a certain caution he felt he should respect.

"I suppose this means no overnighters? No long showers together? No free breakfasts?" he asked.

"I'll make it up to you." Coquettish, she wasn't. But she was more surprised than he was to find the vamp in all women, in her. Surprised and extraordinarily pleased. "I promise. You won't be disappointed."

"Right now? This second? You're going to make it up to me in advance?" He looked worried and brushed at the hand on his inner thigh.

"No. I'll do that later. Right now I'm making up for lost time," she said, rolling on top of him.

He groaned. "How much time?"

"A long time. A *really* long time."

EIGHT

The four summer months of May, June, July, and August are, in many people's minds, the most beautiful season the Pacific coast has to offer. In the winter it can be an ugly place, fierce and desolate. There is never anything gentle about the ocean; the gusty wind and crashing waves see to that. But in the summer when the sky is clear blue and the green-black water meets it on the horizon; when the whitecaps are rolling and the sun dances across the water like something magical; when the wind blows cool against your sun-baked skin and the gulls cry and God smiles down on what He has done, there is a certain calm and serenity to be found.

Rose was never sure if it was its vast expanse or its never-ending rhythm that charmed her soul. Maybe it was the silent cliffs that had bravely faced the ocean's every whim since the beginning of time, and survived. Maybe it was simply the idea that a long empty stretch of pebbled beach was a flimsy barrier between the relative safety of the land and the certain possibility of death at sea.

People had flimsy barriers too. And they were never as safe inside their invisible walls as they thought they were. Rose knew this. The roof of her fortress leaked like a sieve; there were cracks in the walls and gaping holes in the floor. She lived in the constant fear that someone would figure out that her refuge wasn't as impregnable as she led them to believe.

"Oh, I know," Rose shouted, holding her arms out wide in frustration. "I'm the wicked old witch who stole you from your real mother when you were a baby. I keep you prisoner here in my gas station, and I never let you do anything fun. I heard all this when you were six years old, Harley. And I've got news for you, pal, your real mother wouldn't let you do this either."

Gary, walking into the middle of this heated discussion, looked from one Wickum to the other and didn't for an instant doubt they were mother and son. Carrot orange hair that would mellow to a golden copper color with age; two sets of dark green eyes lit with passion; similar pale complexions flushed with anger . . . there was no hocus-pocus involved in this relationship.

They both noticed him standing in the doorway but were too involved to do more than that.

"It's only a week. I don't see what the big deal is," Harley shouted back, slamming the refrigerator door. He was always hanging on the refrigerator door, constantly searching for food.

"The big deal is three fifteen-year-old boys going to Portland alone."

"Paul's sixteen."

"With a brand-new driver's license."

"And his dad's car and his aunt breathing down his neck in Portland. It's not as if we'll be having all *that* much fun."

"Good. Then stay home."

"I wanna go. All my life it's been one long dead summer after the next. I'm bored! I'm going crazy here!"

"What about the Tackle Shack? You've got a job. You have responsibilities. What about that?"

"I asked Aldo if he could spare me for a week. He didn't have a problem with it. In fact, he wants me to stop at some wholesaler's up there and pick up some special lures. He wants to try and check out their new line of tackle . . . pulls over four hundred pounds. Can you believe that?"

Rose went suddenly limp, hooked, so to speak, by his forethought. She was running out of logical arguments.

"Harley, honey," she said, taking a new approach. "I just don't feel easy about this. You're so young and—"

"You didn't feel easy the first time I crossed the street alone, or rode the bus to school, or went hiking with Grampa or rode my bike to Tommy's house or climbed a tree or went on a field trip at school or . . . or anything else I've ever done. Why don't you just lock me in my room and throw away the key? Would you be happy then? I can't wait to get out of this damned town. When I turn eighteen I'm gettin' the hell out of here.

And you can't stop me. I'll never come back. Ever. I'll . . . What?"

He had more to say, but stopped when the anger drained from his mother's face and her eyes glazed over as she stared at him.

If she looked absent, she was. *I'm gettin' the hell out of here. And you can't stop me. I'll never come back. Ever.* The words echoed in her mind, coming from a million miles away. But they weren't Harley's words. They were hers. She was fifteen, like Harley. Her father sat across the room from her in a drunken stupor. Blood trickled down her cheek from a gash on her temple. He'd backhanded her across the face—his most frequent gesture of affection—and she'd fallen, hitting her head on the coffee table. She'd run from the room crying, and by the time the pain had stopped and the anger had set in, he'd lapsed into semiconsciousness—her condition of choice for a confrontation. She'd screamed those exact same words at him and was gone before daylight. Years ago, and yet the bitterness was as deep and fresh as if it happened yesterday.

"What?" he repeated, unfamiliar with this particular mother look.

She sat down at the kitchen table and rubbed her temples with two fingers as if she had a headache. She didn't often act against her instincts, and never did it if Harley started hounding her about something. But the vivid memory of being fifteen in Redgrove, even without a drunken father to contend with, was a powerful argument in his favor.

"Get me the aunt's phone number and let me think about it," she said, defeated.

This small ray of hope was enough for Harley. He grinned and did a little victory dance before he swaggered out of the room, giving Gary a high five as he passed.

Gary approached her with caution. He slid into the chair across the table from her and picked up the clump of fingers she had clutched tightly before her.

"And they say being a garbageman is a rotten job," he said, smiling his understanding when she looked up. "Letting go isn't easy, is it?"

She shook her head. Mother May I? she thought. He had asked and she had given her permission for every baby step he'd ever taken away from her. Now he was asking for giant steps. *Mother, may I leave you? Yes, you may*. She'd been expecting this since the day he was born, preparing for it. How could it be happening so soon? Why did it hurt more than she thought it would?

"He'll be back, Rose. He'll always come back. He loves you."

She looked at him. It wasn't fair that he always seemed to know what she was feeling and thinking. He had no right. He'd be leaving her, too, soon.

"It happens, I guess. Sooner or later. It's supposed to happen," she said, her heart scurrying back into the not-so-solid stronghold she'd built for herself.

Gary opened the front door and walked straight in, seeming not to notice that she'd locked it against him.

"You know what he told me about you once?" he asked, prying her fingers apart so he could hold a hand in each of his. "He said you were the only thing in his life he'd ever been able to count on. You were always there, never too busy for him, always willing to listen. It takes a very mature boy to see that in his mother, and a really good mom to inspire that in her son."

"You think so? He really said that?"

He nodded. "Told me, if I was looking for a good woman, you were the best."

"For crying out loud," she said, pushing his hands away and standing to start their dinner. "I wish he'd stop trying to pawn me off on you."

He laughed. "And here I thought he was waiting for me to make a cash offer on you. Think he'd take my truck in trade?"

"Probably." She turned to the stove, away from him. Would he want his truck back when it was time for him to go too? Or would he want to trade her soul for something new?

"Rose," he said, unaware that he was being figured into the equation that would leave her with nothing. "It'll work out fine. He's a good kid with an excellent head on his shoulders. He just wants to spread his wings a little and test them out."

"I know what he wants to do," she said, peevish. "Could we, ah, change the subject, do you think? I'm getting a headache thinking about all this."

"All right," he said, leaning back in the chair. "That Arts Council Tea you wanted to go to is next week. I have to go down Wednesday, so I thought I'd stay the weekend and wait for you. We can go together."

"You want to go to an Arts Council Tea?"

"Not really, but I thought afterward we could go out to dinner somewhere nice, stay in a fancy hotel. On the way back I could show you my place in Fairfield, if you'd like to see it."

"That sounds . . . nice. Great, in fact. But you don't have to go to the tea. You'd be bored silly," she said. And Justin was already anti-Gary for the time he was taking away from Rose's sculptures. And the Arts Council. Gary would be like an oil slick in this particular sea of society; he simply wouldn't mix well. He was so down-to-earth, and they were so . . . lofty, high-minded, and complicated. "And I've already promised Justin that I'd have dinner with him afterward. To discuss my work."

When there was no invitation extended to him, he nodded and tried to hide his disappointment . . . and jealousy.

"I'm sorry," she said, feeling terrible but knowing it was for the best. She went back to peeling the potatoes.

"No. That's okay. I understand," he said. "I need to hit on a couple of lobbyists in Sacramento anyway. I'll go ahead and stay the weekend and then bop over to Sacramento for a couple days. That'll be a good time to do it. We can meet back here on Wednesday."

"A week," she said aloud, her hands going still mid-peel. A week was a long time. Gary had been traveling back and forth to San Francisco and Sacramento and Fairfield for the past two months, but they hadn't been apart for more than two or three days at a time—and three days was a strain, though their reunions always alleviated that.

Still, maybe a week without him would be good practice for when he was away two weeks. And then three. Then a month. Eventually more.

"A week's a long time," he said, startling her with her own words. "Will you miss me?"

She turned to face him. His knowing smirk didn't bother her one bit.

"Yes. With every inch of me, I'll miss you."

That said, but having very little effect on the dread of seven whole days apart—Rose accepting it as a dry run for the day he never came back, and Gary tortured with thoughts of Rose spending time with another man —the strain of being apart started immediately.

"I told you when I started that there was a chance I might have to miss a few games on account of business. This'll be the first game I've missed, and Joe Spencer can sub for me."

"But this is the Eureka Eagles game," she said, still miffed that he'd felt compelled to point out that she wasn't following through on her swings during practice. "You know how important it is to beat them this year."

"Look, the team won't be any worse off than it was last year when you took second place. We've already beat the Eagles once. If we lose this game, the worst that could happen is that we'll tie for first."

"That's not good enough. We need to beat them."

"Rosemary, I told you," he said, sighing impatiently. "If I could reschedule, I would. But this is my incinerator we're talking about. The Greenpeace people have agreed to meet with us and listen to our proposal. If we can get their support, and if my people in Sacramento do what they're supposed to do, we can start building by Thanksgiving."

"You couldn't tell them that Fridays weren't good for you?"

"For crissake, it's one game. The pitcher's been out twice with menstrual cramps, and Lester missed a game because his mother-in-law's car broke down and he had to go pick her up somewhere. What's the big deal?"

"Nothing. Forget it. Miss the game," she said, walking away, dragging her bat.

They won the game that Gary missed. Lost the next two he played in, and took second place to the Eagles at the end of the season. Again.

"What do you think of this?" she asked, making a grand entrance wearing the dress she'd shopped for all afternoon.

Gary's face lit with approval. It was a simple black sheath dress with spaghetti straps and a short black lace jacket. It was cut low to show a tempting suggestion of her breasts, and high to show off her very shapely legs. With her mother's double strand of faux pearls, she thought the outfit chic, tasteful.

He thought he'd died and gone to heaven.

"I like it," he said, getting to his feet, aching to touch her. "I like it a lot. What's it for?"

"The tea, silly."

"I hate it." He sat down again.

"Why?"

"You shouldn't wear a dress like that unless you're with your grandfather, your son, or me."

She smiled. "You're not jealous, are you?"

"Of course I am." He was serious.

"Really?"

"Yes, really." He stood again, pacing a little. "What? You think I want my woman running all over San Francisco in a skimpy little dress with some other man? Some guy I've never even met?"

"Your woman?" It wasn't that she minded being his woman as much as she minded the way he said it—as if she were his dog or his horse or his piece of meat.

"Some guy I've never met with more in common with her than baseball and books?" he went on. "Some guy I've never met who owns an art gallery, for crissake?"

"I am not your woman."

"What?"

"Well, you make it sound as if you own me. And you don't."

"That's not what I meant. What I meant was—"

"I know what you meant. But you're going to have to trust me. You remember trust, don't you?"

There was nothing worse than falling on your own knife.

He looked away for a second to collect himself.

"I remember trust. But I still wish it were going to be me with you in that dress."

It was the longest Wednesday-to-Wednesday week Rose could remember. And in the end, she'd wished more than anything that she'd taken Gary with her.

However, that wasn't the first thing she told him when he walked into the diner Wednesday evening, just before closing.

The bells over the front door tinkled his tinkle. They rang fifty or sixty times a day, more on the weekend, and they always sounded the same, except when Gary walked in.

Rose hurried from the kitchen to greet him, stopping short when she saw him. Goodness. How could someone get better looking in a week? He seemed bigger too. His presence dominated everything in the room.

He'd stopped to talk to Floyd Bracken, a highway patrol officer who cruised in regularly to fill his thermos with coffee. He was on what he referred to as the Maytag shift, the loneliest shift in the world, patrolling the bleak stretch of Highway 101 from Eureka to the Oregon coast from nine P.M. to nine A.M. He'd pulled Gary over for a burnt-out brake light one night on his way home from her house. They'd hung out together on the side of the road, talking for hours, and had become good friends.

He smiled at something Floyd said, and Rose went weak with longing. When he glanced her way and his smile brightened to a blinding intensity, her heart wiggled and shimmied like a joyful puppy.

"Hi," he said, saying so much more with his eyes.

"Hi," she said, agreeing with him totally.

"How are you?" he asked, making it sound like *I need to touch you. Right now. Let me make love to you. Here on the floor in front of God and everyone.*

"Fine." *Yes, yes!*

"How was your trip?" he asked. Which was really *Hurry and finish so we can leave. I can't wait any longer to be alone with you.*

"All right. I'll tell you about it later." *Right now I'm in a rush.*

If no one noticed the sweltering looks that passed between them or the way their bodies squirmed with excitement if they came within ten feet of each other, they were bound to suspect something was going on when their half-full coffee cups disappeared ten minutes before closing or when Rose stood holding the door open, telling them it was time to close up when the clock on the wall clearly read five minutes to ten. If not at those times, then positively when Gary took them by the arm, smiling and patting them cordially on the back, and all but threw them into the street.

Of course, it was Gladys Ford who reported the next morning that she'd seen Gary's truck streaking away at an incredible speed the night before, and it hadn't returned until after she'd had breakfast.

Still, it was only the two of them who knew that Rose had Gary's shirt open and his fly undone before they pulled onto the dirt road leading to the old farmhouse. He put on the brake and turned off the engine in the front yard, his hands pulling at the buttons on her shirt before the night went silent around them. He pushed her back in the seat, his lips everywhere he could find warm flesh, one hand snaking its way into her blue jeans. She tugged at his khaki slacks, then pushed from the top with both hands pressed to the hot, hot skin of his pelvis.

Their hands groped, their muscles trembled with need. Their breaths mingled in small excited gasps. Finally, when he had but one leg free of her pants, he pulled her forward, lifting her onto his lap and his urgent desire. There was a simultaneous moan of relief and a moment of utter ecstasy before the tiniest movement excited them again. He lifted his head from the back of the seat to suckle first one breast, then the other, dragging one pleasured groan after another from deep in her chest. She held his head close, her fingers fisted in his thick dark hair as she impaled herself again and again, harder and harder, deeper and deeper until the clamor within her exploded in the night, scattering tiny fragments of her in the wind, to float weightless.

When he could, he held her, stroking her back, soaking her in through his fingertips. With his eyes closed and his emotions close to the surface, he promised himself he'd never be away from her that long again. Never. And certainly not because of his pride.

He could have come back Sunday; his appointments in Sacramento hadn't been till Tuesday. Two days he could have been near her, but his pride and jealousy had kept him at home, in an empty house, with nothing but his stubbornness to keep him company.

"I missed you so much," she said, her face in the bend of his neck, her breath warm against his skin. "I should have let you come with me." Then she added, "It was awful."

"What? The whole thing was awful? Or being without me was awful?"

"Yes. Both."

"Why?" he asked, trying to look at her by the dashboard lights. "What happened?"

She moved her head a bit. "Not now. Later. I don't want to spoil this."

He smiled. "My legs are going to sleep anyway. Come on. Let's go inside. We can do it again. Right this time. Slow, the way you like it."

"I like all of it. Every way. Any way I can get it."

"I've noticed that," he said, handing her a wad of clothes. He helped her pull the other leg of her jeans off in the close confines of the cab and watched as she slipped her panties back on. He grinned. "Think someone's going to see you streaking to the house?"

"No," she said, her smile bright in the dull light. "I like it when you take them off."

There was no sleep for the wicked that night. They were cold by the time they reached the bedroom, stopping in the kitchen for a beer and a diet soda. The house was equipped with two hot water tanks, and they used up both of them in a long, leisurely, intimate shower.

"How do you like it when I take your towel off?" he asked, his arms circling her from behind as she brushed out her wet hair, his hands resting on the rolled corners of the towel above her breast.

"I don't know. Try it and see," she said, her gaze meeting his in the mirror. They stared at each other as his fingers slowly loosened the towel, pulled it away from her body, and dropped it on the floor. He pressed his nakedness to her back, cupping her breasts in his hands, then slowly slid them lower and lower. Her breath caught in her throat. Her heart raced out of control. When her neck grew weak and her head fell back against his shoulder, he turned her in his arms and kissed her, and this time their loving was slow and sweet and heart-wrenching.

"I like it when you miss me," he said sometime later, an undeniable gloating in his voice. "I thought you were insatiable before, but this is amazing. You're shameless."

"I thought you said you liked it," she said, so spent, her words were slurred.

"I do."

"Then quit complaining. If you can't handle it . . ."

"I can handle it," he said, rolling quickly from his back to wrap her in his arms. "I think," he added softly.

They lay quiet, relishing the sensation of skin on skin.

"Tell me why it was awful," he said, muttering as if he were asking for a bedtime story; as if he were about to have happy dreams knowing that she hadn't had a good time without him.

"It wasn't awful," she said, caressing his thick muscled arm with soothing strokes. "I was awful."

He pulled back to look at her.

"What does that mean? How were you awful?"

"It's hard to explain."

"I'm listening."

She sighed heavily, wondering where to start. Her mind jumped over the lunch she'd shared with Justin. He'd scolded her for neglecting her work over the past few months. She hadn't. She'd tried to explain that she'd been working regular hours on it; that Gary wasn't standing in her way; that he actually encouraged her by bringing take out to the house so she didn't have to stop and cook, and hauling Harley here and there to give her more time with the sculptures. Once again she'd tried to make him see that it wasn't a matter of time that was holding her up, it was the lack of desire that was holding her back. She didn't like the big sculptures, didn't enjoy them, didn't love them.

Her mind blocked out the intimate dinner they'd dallied over after the tea. She had decided it would be best to forget that Justin had come on to her, tried to kiss her, touched her as if he had a thousand hands. Her shock was nothing to the anger she felt with his explanation. If she seemed less distant, less untouchable, more like a warm, open woman than a beautiful cool statue to him, it was entirely Gary's doing, not his. And if this new woman Justin saw had anything worth giving, she'd be giving it to Gary first. Thank you very much.

No, it was the hours between the two meals on Saturday that were awful.

"Justin calls them the Art World," she said, starting slowly. "Or sometimes the World of Art. He says they're everybody who's anybody worth knowing, who deals in art on the West Coast. Gallery owners from everywhere, collectors, brokers, fundraisers, benefactors, artists—with and without names. Special people. Rich people. Powerful people.

"Justin introduced me to the ones he thought were important. And me? I smiled and said all the right words and did all the right things. I sipped on a glass of wine I didn't want and listened to them shred the work of one artist after another. I was like someone I didn't know. All these people who couldn't draw a straight line to save their souls, but who have somehow set themselves up as the be-all and end-all authorities on good art, and I was pretending to be one of them.

"I stood there and nodded like a dummy," she said, her speech coming faster and more heated. "I didn't defend anyone. I let Justin go on and on about my sculptures, as if I were proud of them. I stood there in those tight high heels and hoped with all my heart that those people would approve of me and my work. The work I did to please them, not myself. I walked out of that fancy reception hall feeling as if I'd been sucked dry. Like an empty coffee pot with nothing left but the gooky black dregs."

Hearing this, Gary was glad he hadn't gone. It really didn't sound like his cup of tea, as it were.

"You know," he said, his tone thoughtful. "I don't think you should be beating yourself up about this. Nobody likes it, but it seems to be a part of life. Everywhere you turn, there are puffed-up people who don't know diddly about what's going on, and there they are holding all the strings, making all the rules, screaming with the loudest voice. I have to deal with them all the time. And I don't think anybody really knows what to do with them. There's no standard practice for getting around them. You put up with them. You go along with them as far as you can. You use them, because they're using you to make themselves seem important."

"But I feel like such a hypocrite," she said, miserable.

"I know. You're supposed to. It's all part of the game in the beginning."

She looked at him, confused.

"If you follow your conscience and fight them, you're dead before you ever get started. That's where their power lies. If you don't play by their rules, they simply lock you out and you never get in. But once you're in, it's your guilt and those feelings of fraud and deception that they count on to keep you submissive, which perpetuates their power over you."

"I don't think I can live like that, Gary."

"You don't have to," he said, pressing a kiss to her temple, giving himself a pat on the back for his excellent taste in women. "Didn't we already say they were know-nothing know-it-alls? Then you be smart. Beat 'em at their own game. Do what you have to do to get in, and get to the top. But keep your perspective. Don't get sucked into their way of thinking. Remember what's really important in your life and be true to that. Then when you have your own power inside the group, you stomp on these people." He paused. "It's a game, Rose. Not a fun game, but a game nonetheless."

She sighed. "I still think I should have said something. Several people had pieces on display. Why do they have to be so vocal with their opinions? If something doesn't appeal to them, couldn't they simply walk away without tearing it apart? They mutilated some of those pieces. Pieces someone put time and sweat and blood into." She hesitated. "They're going to chew me up and spit me out."

"At least you'll be bleeding inside on the floor instead of outside in the dirt. It's no consolation, I know, but you can try again if you play your cards right," he said. "You don't always have to speak you mind. You don't have to help them tear anything apart; you don't have to agree with them. Just don't fight them until you know you can win."

A thought occurred to her, and she twisted her neck to get a good look at him.

"You play this game all the time, don't you? With your landfills and incinerators. Only for you it's the government and the environmentalists and property owners."

"It's almost exactly the same game. But in my case I've got a clock to beat. And when my time runs out, *everyone* will be powerless. No one will be able to stop what will happen."

The light of the sun dissolved the dark film of night. Shadows faded to gray and hid from the daylight hours as they lay in each other's arms pondering life, the world, and the roles they played in it.

NINE

She was crazy. She knew it. But that didn't stop her from racing across the street on her lunch break to fetch the mail.

"He's only been gone a day, and he called you last night to tell you he'd gotten there safely," Gary said, his ignorance sticking out all over. Clearly he'd never been a mother.

"She knows that," Lu said. She was leaning on her side of the lunch counter, watching with the others as Rose frantically sorted the junk mail from the bills, looking for a postcard from Harley.

When she came across a particular envelope, frowned at it a moment, then finished her useless search and went back to it, she had everyone's interest piqued.

"You didn't find one, did you?" Lu asked, thinking she'd grossly underestimated Harley's attachment to his mother.

"No. Not from Harley. But this one's from the San Francisco Patrons of Fine Arts Ball Committee."

"Well, open it. Open it," was the general accord.

"Oh no," she said, peeking into the envelope before she pulled out four tastefully printed cream-colored tickets.

"What are they?" Lucy Flannary asked, her chin resting on her fists over a glass of cherry cola.

"Tickets to the ball," Rose said, sounding ill. "The Patrons' Ball. Do you have any idea how much these tickets cost?"

"Send 'em back," Emma Motley, postmistress, said. "It's against the law to—"

"Oh, I'm going to send them back, all right." Rose broke in. She was miffed. "I've been telling Justin for months that I couldn't afford to go to this, so he takes it upon himself to send me tickets. Well, I can't accept these. It's too much."

"Wait a second," Gary said, setting his coffee mug on the counter. "Think this through. If he wants you to go so bad, he must think it's pretty important."

"It's not. The whole thing is boring," she said, reconsidering the tickets. "I pawned an arm and a leg two years ago to go. The food was terrible. Justin thought the tea and this ball were the best places to start getting my name out before the Amateur Art Show at Fennway's Gallery in August."

"You're showing your sculptures." It was a half question, half statement.

"Maybe. If they're finished. If they're good enough."

"Then the artsy fella is right," Lucy said, passing down her judgment. "Even vague name recognition is better than no recognition at all."

"And if you make an impression on one or two people and they like you, so much the better when they see your work," Emma said. "They'll say nice things about you, even if they hate what you've done."

Rose's gaze rose to Gary's.

"It's part of the game, isn't it?" He nodded. She filled her cheeks with a deep sigh until the air broke through her lips. She chewed the lower one as she thought it over. Finally she held up one ticket. "Okay. I'll send three of them back and pay him for this one."

"How come he sent four?" Danny O'Brian asked, not all that interested in the conversation to begin with —he was having a Rubbermaid sale *and* a Craftmaster tool sale *and* a lawn and garden sale all at once and couldn't get involved right now. But he did see the disparity of sending four expensive ball tickets when only one was needed.

"Maybe he wants you to bring the whole family," Lu suggested with a humorous smirk, as if she were picturing Earl in a tuxedo.

Rose was frowning at the elegant invitations, seeing Justin's error for the first time. Why *had* he sent four tickets? Maybe there had been some sort of mix-up. Still . . . Harley all dressed up and Earl . . .

"Like they'd come," she muttered.

"I'd go," Gary said, his eyes bright with enthusiasm, hinting heavily for an invitation.

Naturally, no one but Rose was surprised to hear

that he considered himself a part of the family. Not now that their dates sometimes ended at eight in the morning.

"Oh no, you'd hate it. I'd never put you through that," she said, beginning to feel uneasy.

"I've been to things like this before," he said. "I even own my own tux."

The two ladies having coffee to his left were more impressed than Rose.

"You'd hate it," she insisted.

"No I wouldn't. And I can help Earl and Harley rent their duds. Oh! What about a limo? I could rent one for the night. That would be fun. The four of us could make a night of it."

"Oh, right. Earl? As if we wouldn't have to gag and hog-tie him first?"

"How do you know that? Maybe he's always wanted to go to something like this. Have you ever asked him?"

"Well, no, but . . ."

"You really ought to ask him," Emma said, nodding judiciously. "Opportunities like this don't come in the mail every day, you know."

"That's true," Lucy added. "And as I recall, ol' Earl was a dasher as a young man. My oh my, I remember him being such a handsome young fella. With those wide shoulders. He'd come in from the lumber camp all slicked back and smellin' fine. . . ."

"Earl?" Rose and Lu asked together.

"Sure. Course, I had my Martin, but your grampa set many a young girl's hearts to fluttering in his time."

Rose simply stared at her for a few seconds before Gary distracted her.

"There, you see?" he said. "You should at least ask him."

She considered it a moment longer.

"What about Harley?"

"A limo ride? A fancy night out in San Francisco? Food everywhere?"

It did seem to be right up Harley's alley. That left Gary. How comfortable would a garbageman be at a snooty ball for art buffs? Of course, in a tuxedo he'd look like everyone else. Better than most, actually. He could pretend to be anything he wanted.

"You don't really want to go to this," she said. "You're just being nice, and you don't need to be. Really. If it's the extra ticket you're worried about, Lu can use it. You'd love to go, wouldn't you, Lu?"

"Actually," she said, noting a tourist at the register wanting to pay his bill, "that's the weekend I asked you to work for me. Jimmy and I are going down to the city. We're doing Fisherman's Wharf."

"Well, that cuts it," Rose said, relieved. "None of us can go. Unless you'd like to go without me?" She was looking at Gary, who was shaking his head and ready to protest.

"You can go. We'll all go to San Francisco that weekend," Lu said, walking over to the register, smiling.

"You're closing the diner? In the summertime? On a weekend?"

What *would* the tourists do?

"Course not." Everyone waited to hear her idea while she made change for the man. "I'll get Clair Lucus to come in and cook the way she used to, and Harley's little friend, Heather, can earn a little extra pocket money waiting tables. It'll reinforce the importance of a college education on her."

"Oh no, that's crazy. I don't really want to go anyway. And paying extra to have Clair and—"

"It's a done deal," Lu said, breaking in on Rose's excuses. "You go out and buy yourself a pair of red shoes, and let Mr. Talldarkandhandsome here show you how to kick up your heels. This old hole can survive two days without us." She smirked. "You two be sure to get two rooms, now." A pregnant pause. "And make Earl and Harley sleep in the other one."

Somewhere in the middle of the snickers and sidelong glances and bobbing heads, it was settled. One one-hundredth of the population of Redgrove was going to San Francisco for the weekend.

By the time Harley arrived home the next week—in one piece, a validated miracle to be sure—Rose still hadn't found a dress to wear to the ball. All three men in her life disappeared for an afternoon and returned after supper with two rented tuxedos. A traditional black one for Harley and a nattier job with black pants and a maroon jacket for Earl, who, it was told later, had tried on twelve different styles and colors before he found one to suit his personality.

However, the most arresting episodes during this

period were the sudden and staggering increases in her tip money; Lucy Flannary's offer to make her a dress despite the short time frame; the special visit from Gladys Ford's daughter, Betty, to loan her a genuine diamond chip cocktail ring that her mother thought Rose might be able to use; and several offers to loan her an antique wedding dress or a worn-once prom gown or a beaded handbag.

It was a strange feeling to look into the eyes of these people that she'd faced in shame and guilt so often in the past, and find nothing but goodwill and encouragement. Odder still was the sensation that it wasn't something new, and yet this was the first time she'd noticed it.

"I don't know what to say," she said, her voice soft with wonder. Lu had insisted she follow her home that night after work. There in the uncomfortably neat, clean living room of the little house she owned along the highway, Lu presented her with a cream-colored dream of a dress that glowed with the rich dull shine of pearls and yards and yards of gossamer chiffon that seemed to float more like a cloud than a skirt. It looked like an angel's gown, the thought struck her as tears pooled in her eyes. "It's too beautiful."

"Don't be silly. And don't you cry," Lu said sternly. "It's almost as old as Harley. I let it take up space in my closet because I knew it would come back into style someday; everything does eventually."

"But Lu . . ." she said, feeling she ought to decline the offer to borrow it, knowing it would be too stupid not to take it, wishing she had the words to express herself. "You should wear it. For Jimmy."

She laughed. "And have him rip it getting it off me? I don't think so. He's too young to appreciate a dress like this. No, this dress with your pale skin and that red hair of yours . . . mm-mm . . . you'll be something to savor and enjoy. And trust me, because I know men, Gary knows how to savor and enjoy." She paused. "Am I right or am I right?"

Rose lowered her eyes and smiled self-consciously. If the way he made love was an indicator, he did know.

"When did you wear it, Lu? What was the occasion?" she asked impulsively, having never come this close to Lu's past before.

"I never did," she said. She sounded wistful and looked a bit surprised, as if she'd always meant to wear it but never got around to it. "It was a gift. Sort of a going-away gift, I guess."

That was all she said, and Rose couldn't bring herself to pry, though she desperately wanted to.

"Everyone's been so nice," she said, changing the subject to lighten a dark tension creeping into the air around them. "Lucy, Gladys, Janice, everyone. And now you. I feel like Cinderella with all these fairy godmothers."

Closing the door firmly on her past, Lu smiled. "We love you," she said. Lu had a way of making things seem so simple. Still, there was a moment of caution before she went on. "Emma once told me that she used to watch you growing up. Wild, unkept, uncared for. She said she wanted to steal you away to a safe place and raise you as her own. 'Love you to death' was what she said. That was when I first came here and I didn't know much about you, but . . ."

"But what?"

"But she wasn't the only one. Everyone watched what happened to you after your mother died. Knew about your daddy, saw the bruises, prayed for you when you ran away. They knew how you felt when Harley was born and stood back in awe and admiration and pride as you held your head high and did your best to raise him." She hesitated once more. "This town is very proud of you, Rose. Of the person you've become. They want to see you happy."

She left Lu's house a short time later, confused and more than a little worried. It was a lot to take in. All those years of carefully avoiding the expressions on her neighbors' faces, of being too prickly to touch, too proud to approach, too angry and hurt to let herself feel anything else. Had it been an appalling waste of time and energy . . . and life?

All those years of believing that they were looking down on her. Had it been Rose looking down on Rose? On who she was and where she came from, and nothing more than that?

All those years of resenting the meddling and the gossip, designing her life to avoid them, never seeing them as attempts to help or to show concern . . . Had she really believed herself to be so unworthy, so unlovable?

It was easier to see in retrospect. The words, the gestures, the people. She'd known them all her life.

They all enjoyed a good goof-up; they loved to tease one another. But when the chips were down, when one of them was hurt or bleeding silently within, they all felt it. They knew. They rallied and gave support. But she hadn't seen it because she'd been too ashamed, too caught up in her own guilt and humiliation to recognize it.

She lay awake for hours that night wishing Gary weren't away on business. She wanted to share her discovery with him. He'd be back the following afternoon. Would he be able to perceive the new, fragile self-confidence she could feel sprouting in her soul? Would he be able to feel the lightness in her heart she was experiencing? Years earlier she'd laid the foundation of her life on the assumption that love wasn't meant to be a part of it. Would he sense the slow reconstruction taking place inside her? Would he be willing to help?

The big day was upon them. Lu waved and honked as she drove out of town, Jimmy looking equally eager on the passenger side of the small compact car. The three of them—Rose, Harley, and Grampa Earl—stood behind the plate glass window of the garage with their garment bags and their brown-paper-shopping bag overnight luggage, waiting for Gary to arrive in the limousine. It was raining, of course.

Both Harley and Earl had been to San Francisco before, and insisted that blue jeans, work boots, and filthy high-top sneakers were the things to wear that day if she wasn't going to let them wear their tuxedos until that evening. Rose, on the other hand, was wearing a smart going-to-town business suit.

"Harley, if you belch out loud between now and the time we get back, I promise, I will break your neck. I want you to stand up straight and tall. Watch your language. If you see something you don't like on the buffet table, keep your mouth shut. No one will want to hear you compare it to anything dead, mutilated, or rejected by the body. Did you bring those cigarettes I bought you?" she asked, addressing Earl now. "You probably won't be able to smoke inside the building anyway, but I'd much rather have you doing that than wandering around looking for a good place to spit. You go anywhere near a potted plant, and I'll know what you're doing," she warned him. To them both she added, "And for goodness sake, if they have artwork displayed, don't talk to anyone about it. You never know who you're talking to at these things. Just . . . try to stay out of trouble. Smile a lot. Have a good time."

"Right," Harley said, as if he'd been writing it all down and had very little room for the have-fun part.

Why on earth had Justin sent them tickets? she wondered, not for the first time.

"Oh, there it is," she said, pointing, clutching the garment bag close to her stomach to ease her nerves. "Don't play with all the gadgets, now. It's a limousine, not a space shuttle. You've been in a car before; this isn't any different."

Well, it was a lot different, and Rose was just as tempted to check out the little refrigerator and see if she could get *The Beverly Hillbillies* on the TV as Harley was. She didn't, however. She sat with her hands in her lap, pretending to be above it all.

It was important that she not appear to be backward or unsophisticated. She wanted to make a good impression. Justin's Art World had certain standards, and Gary was right, she didn't have to approve of them, but she did have to live up to them, or at least seem to, for now.

Thank God for Gary, she thought, sliding her fingers across the plush upholstery to touch his, to feel them instantly taken in strength, warmth, and security. They smiled at each other.

Gary knew the importance of playing the game. He understood it. She thought the limo was a bit much, especially with Earl and Harley acting like a couple of sightseers. But it certainly was awe-inspiring—and that couldn't hurt.

But when she was ushered into the suite of rooms he'd reserved at the Essex Hotel, where the ball was being held, she knew that not only did Gary know how to play the game, he knew how to play it well.

Still and all, there were the nervous snakes in her stomach to contend with. What if the chic elite of San Francisco didn't like her? What if they found her too dull and small-town to believe she had any talent? What if she accidently insulted one of them? What if she spilled something down the front of her dress? Or worse, down the front of one of the society's preferred? What if she tripped, fell off her high-heeled shoes, and landed flat on her face in the middle of the room?

"You won't," Gary told her, listening patiently to her fears. She had long since driven Earl and Harley from the suite with her constant bedeviling on ball behavior. They'd gone off to explore the rest of the elegant old hotel and left Gary to coax her into a hot, relaxing tub of bubbles. "We'll travel the perimeter of the room instead of cutting through the middle, and if you feel faint or start to teeter on your shoes, you can reach out and hang on to me," he said, teasing her gently.

He was sitting beside the big marble bathtub, sponging warm water over her shoulders. It was scented with some strange but pleasant exotic fragrance, but it didn't seem to be soothing her the way the bouquet of roses always could.

"I'm being an idiot, aren't I?" she asked, sliding lower into the bubbles, letting the water from the sponge flow over her troubled breast. "I shouldn't let anything but Harley mean this much to me, should I?"

"Well . . . maybe me," he suggested, taking no offense.

She sighed, turned her head to look at him, and smiled in a fashion that both asked forgiveness and agreed with his wisdom.

"What would I be like if you weren't here with me?" she wondered aloud, her voice indicating the extent of the imagined disaster.

"You'd be like Rosemary Wickum. A little nervous inside, composed and beautiful on the outside," he said, placing his lips on her warm wet shoulder.

"Mmm," she hummed, closing her eyes, letting sweet warm waves of excitement pass along her body. "I thought Justin was crazy to send all those tickets at first. Now I think it was pretty wonderful of him."

"Mmm. Remind me to thank him."

"Remind *me* to thank *you.*"

"For what?"

"For being here."

"When?"

"Now."

"No, I mean, when do you want me to remind you to thank me?"

She opened her eyes and smiled into his eyes.

"Any time you want," she said, liking the fact that they always seemed to be not only on the same track, but on the same train, traveling in the same direction, proceeding to the same destination.

"Like . . . now?" His brows bobbed up and down lecherously. "They say that giving thanks is good for the soul."

He kissed her.

"And making love is a good tension release? Don't they say that too?"

She kissed him back.

"No. They say good sex is a great release for tension," he said, correcting her with a soft voice as his hands slid below bubble level. "Making love is a cure-all for whatever ails you."

"I say we go for the cure-all," she said, her voice catching as her hands covered his over each of her breasts. "Are you going to undress and come in, or shall I get out?"

"Yes," he said, slipping into the room-for-many tub,

clothes and all. Her shocked giggle barely escaped before his mouth closed over hers, his hands skimming over her body.

And the mess of wet clothes and towels and loose pools of water on the floor after their lovemaking? Well, it was nothing compared to the chaos they left behind getting ready for the ball.

When Rose finally emerged from the bathroom amidst a cloud of powder and rose-scented perfume, she looked for all the world to see, like something ethereal in Lu's made-in-heaven dress.

"Wow." Harley was the only one who could manage to speak. Earl and Gary stood gaping and dazed.

"You all look so handsome," she said, warm and blushing during their astonished inspection. "I say we skip the ball and just stand here admiring each other."

"Not me," Gary said. "I want to hang you on my arm and go downstairs to show you off. You're stunning."

She simpered uncomfortably, unused to such distinct and spirited praise. She looked up when his proffered arm came into view. She questioned the adoration in his eyes for a split second, then smiled and basked in it. Then they both glanced at Earl when he let loose a loud barking cough.

Clearly the oldest and, in his absolute opinion, the most dashing man in the room, he took no notice of Gary and swaggered across the room like a young lumberjack to take Rose's arm himself.

Without a word, and with a great deal of affection

for the old fart, she tucked her hand in the bend of his arm, stood a little taller to meet his fine height, and allowed him to lead her away.

Never one to hold a grudge for long, Gary grinned and waved Harley through the door ahead of him.

TEN

It was a fairy-tale evening.

It was a magical time touched by pixies and sprites.

It was a night that excited the senses and soothed the soul. For when the elevator doors opened, the first thing they saw was a bright red and yellow Alexander Calder creation dangling poised and balanced on the far side of the lobby. A large anteroom had been converted into a small museum of select and precious sculptures, with everything from a pure, extremely simple and totally lovely piece of José de Rivera's construction series to a welded metal configuration by John Chamberlain to an assemblage by Jasper Johns, who had a real knack for painting everything he could find bronze and giving it a title—his paintbrushes, toothbrushes, and flashlight for example.

A David Smith classic in stainless steel took Rose's breath away. She hadn't recovered it when she spotted the Ibram Lassaw piece in bronze alloys, copper, and steel. Poor baby, she was weak kneed and drooling by the time she got to the 1915 Lipchitz bronze. Gary, however, gravitated toward the sculptures with identifiable parts—the James Seawright composition of metal, plastic, and electronic parts, and the box constructions of Joseph Cornell. Earl—surprise, surprise—was completely taken with a Jean Dubuffet mixed-media collage and wanted to buy it, until Rose took a guesstimate on a price for him. Even Harley found an original masterpiece by Harold Tovish that he could relate to. He said it looked like the metal man in *Terminator 2.*

She took the opportunity to give him a brief explanation of ceramic-shell casting, sand casting, and the *cire-perdue,* or lost-wax, process used by Tovish to create his sculpture and was gratified by the semi-interested nod she received for her efforts.

It was a moment-to-moment, revelation-to-revelation, marvel-to-marvel event—and they hadn't yet left the anteroom.

A night unlike any Rose had ever dreamed of, it was as rare and unique as—as a glass slipper, no doubt. The ballroom had the rich warm glow of gold on white; crystal twinkled and tinkled all around. Glorious gowns shimmered and jewels glistened. The smiles were dazzling.

It was a phenomenon so different from the last ball Rose had attended. Gracious. Grand. Graceful and surprisingly cordial.

Or . . . perhaps it wasn't so different?

She had firm recall of feeling toadlike compared to the beautiful women around her. Dark and warty amidst the gaiety, frightened and prepared to make an escape if anyone approached her. Alone and lonely, with no grisly old face to nod recognition from across the room, no warmhearted gaze to glance at for reassurance, no heavy-metal mouth to grin at her from the buffet table.

Tonight she felt beautiful, charming, and witty. Accepted and loved. *She* was the difference. She began to perceive the power of the possibilities. They surged through her veins like adrenaline, filling her with determination and a small sample of faith in the future.

Gary wasn't much of a line dancer or a two-stepper, but he could waltz like a member of the Welk family. A-one and a-two and a-off he'd go, stepping in squares but spinning her in circles until her mind reeled. Chandeliers glimmered from above, and she and Gary giggled together, blithe and breathless. The orchestra played music that made their hearts light and their eyes shine. Good food and drink brought out the best in everyone.

Even Justin, arriving more than an hour late, took note of the highly festive atmosphere. Of course, he had only one thing to talk about, but even then, he was enthusiastic and upbeat.

"To create shapes which triumph over insipid stereotypes, the artist must utilize his individual sensitivities, contrive a unique and personal representation, and remain vulnerable to new experiences. Develop, in short, those characteristics which we are in awe of in children," he was telling Gary after a brief introduction and his comment on the evening, which went something like "Great time, very impressive, very interesting."

"We are continually challenged with things as they are, not as we dream them to be," he continued in the same breath. "But to see things as they are, to appreciate the subtleties which differentiate each element and particle of time, requires a process of visualizing which has no room for preconceptions and prejudice. We become, then, attentive to relationships, rather than details and time separately, and we give harmony and perception to vision.

"The wide range of materials and complex expertise integral to an industrial society has produced advantages for the sculptor of today which would have been inconceivable at any other time. . . ."

A quick glance at Gary, and Rose could see that his eyes were fixed and dim with boredom and disinterest. Not that she could blame him. The music and lightheartedness around them didn't lend itself to a verbal art lesson. Justin's good intentions notwithstanding.

". . . To contrive a finished piece of sculpture requires a perception of solidarity with the method, an appreciation of the change in forces, a realization of the restrictions, and a deep admiration for the excellence of material and method. . . ."

"Justin," she said, breaking in as he took a second breath. "You haven't asked me to dance yet."

He looked at her, confused.

"That *is* what people do at balls, you know. They dance."

"Oh. Yes, of course, how dull of me," he said. Then, looking at Gary, he added, "Business, business, always business. But you don't get to be a man in my position without a few sacrifices. However, in this case, I believe Rose is right. Time to slow down and enjoy a waltz or two. May I?"

Gary all but pushed Rose into his arms with a too-magnanimous smile. Having met Justin had put any fears he might have had about her interest in him to rest. Killed them dead, in fact. He went off to find Earl, who had last been seen with a tall, willowy brunette in his arms. He was dying to know if the old man was actually asking women to dance or merely jerking his head toward the dance floor and grunting.

"I must admit that this antipollution person you've been seeing is doing something right. I've always thought you a striking woman, Rose," Justin said, dancing her slowly back and forth near the center of the room, where everyone was sure to see him. "But you have this new inner glow that's very attractive. So appealing."

"I'm sure it's this dress," she said, half serious. "I've been expecting to sprout wings all evening. Don't you think it looks like an angel costume? I'm pretty sure it has something to do with the glow you're seeing."

"If it is an angel's costume, it's simply because you're wearing it."

Oh boy. She had hoped to avoid a repeat of their last meeting.

"Well, I wouldn't be in it at all if it weren't for you," she said, changing the subject. "I should have called to thank you, but I wanted to wait until tonight. Until I could do it face-to-face. It's the nicest thing anyone's ever done for me."

"It was my pleasure," he said, smiling. "Whatever it was, I'm sure I was glad to do it."

"The tickets," she said, floored. How nice it must be to have so much money that giving away a thousand dollars' worth of ball tickets could be so easily forgotten, she speculated. "Remember? You sent me four of them."

"Tickets to what?"

"To this," she said, thinking him dumber than a barrel of hair after all. "You can't have forgotten. Remember I told you that I couldn't afford the tickets, so I wasn't planning to come, and then you sent me four tickets in the mail?"

"Four? Why would I send four? That's . . . darling, that's a thousand dollars."

"I know. That's why—" She stopped. "You didn't send them."

"Well, if it was the nicest thing anyone's ever done for you, I wish I had. That's a lot of money to pay for something you can't insure, but if—"

"You didn't send them," she said again.

"I'm afraid not."

"Then who?" she wondered aloud, her feet stopping as if it were impossible for her to determine the likely prospects and dance at the same time.

"The pollution person?"

Gary? A long shot, but . . . "Why didn't he say anything? For weeks I've been telling everyone how terrific you were to . . ."

A familiar sensation swept over her, and a smile tugged at her lips. She'd walked into another one of

Gary's little traps. He'd let her go on and on, singing Justin's praises, knowing in the end that she'd find out who really sent the tickets and how truly terrific her real champion was.

Not that she hadn't known all along, she thought, glancing around the room for him, eager to show the proper proponent her appreciation in a manner she wouldn't have shown to Justin.

That's when it happened. When it started, anyway.

With that seventh sense that a mother develops during gestation—that same instinct that alerts her to missing cookies before dinner; that warns her she's getting a raspberry when she turns away; that tells her when to get the truth, the whole truth, and nothing but the truth and when a major misdemeanor is in the making—she took heed, cocking her head like a doe in a forest, watchful, searching for Gary, she thought, but instead happening to catch sight of Harley removing a glass of wine from a passing waiter's tray.

It was not a huge crime, and certainly not one she shouldn't have expected—what with young boys being what they were. But it was a violation that he shouldn't repeat if he didn't want to be falling-down drunk before the end of the evening.

"Justin, will you excuse me?" she said, keeping an eye on the felon as he slipped back into the shadows with his spoils.

"You can thank him later," he said, unaware that she had metamorphosed from a grateful lover to a correctional officer before his eyes. "I want to introduce you to some important people with deep pockets. Otis Remson in particular. Very into large sculptures. Owns two of Herbert Ferber's."

"All right, but it'll have to wait a second or two. I just saw Harley . . ."

"Your child? He's here?" He made it sound as if she'd brought along the family dog.

"I had four tickets," she said defensively. "I thought . . ."

No, Gary had suggested they all go together. And despite what she'd just witnessed, it was a suggestion she couldn't regret taking. In the past two weeks she'd discovered more about herself and Harley and Earl as individuals, and as a family, than she had in—in all her life.

They loved her. *Lots* of people loved her and cared about her life. It was still an odd notion to maneuver around in her head, but her heart was already settling into it comfortably, delightedly. Having them with her that night made her feel as if she belonged; it was a reminder that she did belong and could belong anywhere she happened to be.

". . . I thought it was your wonderful and most generous idea for me to bring them along," she said, finishing her sentence in a light he could use to make himself look better. Or not.

"This is no place for a boy his age," he said, ignoring the light. "What if he does something . . . adolescent?"

"What if he does?" she asked, prickling as any mother might, despite what she'd observed moments ago. "And he's not a boy or a child. He's fifteen. He's a young man. A very bright young man, and he knows how to behave himself." Sort of. "If he happens to make a mistake due to his inexperience, who would hold that against him?"

"Perhaps not him, darling, but certainly you for bringing him. Whatever made you think of it?"

Gary. With something as simple as pulling up a shade, he'd shown her life outside herself. He'd let her see that there were people standing nearby who wanted to be a part of her life, and all she had to do was smile and wave them in.

She smiled now. "The devil made me do it, and, frankly, I'm glad he did. Don't worry so much. Everything will work out fine," she said, actually believing it for a moment. The music was slowing to an end. "Where will you be? I'll come find you in a few minutes, but I really should check in with Harley."

Disgruntled, he made a vague gesture to the far side of the room and let her go. Her maternal radar kicked in, and within minutes she spotted the back of her son's red head.

"Hi, honey, how are you doing?" she asked, waiting to catch him with his lips to the glass. The startled sputter was gratifying, the cough was appeasing, and the hurried and difficult gulping noise in his throat as he cleared away the last few drops of evidence was well worth the trip across the room, if the sour look on his face when he turned around was any indication.

"Mom. Hi." He didn't bother to hide the glass, he'd already seen the look in her eyes.

"You know," she said in a deceptively soft and pleasant tone of voice that Harley understood immediately. "Your real mother probably wouldn't mind that." She indicated the wineglass with one all-knowing and undeniable finger. "But if I catch you doing it again, she won't be able to recognize you when she finally comes to steal you back. Is that understood?"

"Yes, ma'am."

She could see it was.

"Did you like the way it tastes?" she asked, with as much curiosity as understanding.

"Not really," he said, aware of the role alcohol played in his personal history. "It's bitter. Beer's better, but it has a . . . an aftertaste, you know?" He screwed up his face.

"When did you have beer?" He gave her a don't-be-stupid look, and she remembered what it was like to be fifteen. "Oh yes. I forgot. Well," she sighed fatalistically, "you're a smart young man, honey, and you're getting too old for me to keep you from doing what you really want to do—you'll always be able to find a way round me. But you're also the one who will always have to pay the consequences for your actions. If not with me, with someone else."

"I know."

"Okay," she said, praying he truly did know. "Now, what have you done with your grampa? We should both be keeping an eye on *him.*"

Harley chuckled. "I haven't seen him in an hour. Think he took someone up to our suite? Want me to go check?"

"Oh, you." She bumped him with her elbow. He

loved seeing her so happy. "Just keep your eyes open. Are you having any fun, honey?"

"Yeah. This whole thing is really out there."

"Okay." She knew 'out there' was a good thing. "Well, I'm supposed to go meet a few people, and I need to find Gary. Did you know he sent the tickets?" He shook his head, smiling. Being Gary's guest was a whole lot better than being Justin's. "Well, he did. Have you seen him in the last few minutes?" She was scanning the crowd.

"Nope."

"If you do, will you tell him I'm looking for him? But don't say anything about the tickets, all right? And behave yourself."

"I will. Is it okay to eat more than once?"

"At these prices, you can eat till they're down to their last soda cracker. Just don't take the last of anything, that's rude."

Walking through the crowd, she was alert to the fact that she was being noticed. People were looking at her, nodding her way when they happened to make eye contact, smiling politely.

Maybe it's the dress, she thought, feeling pretty and basking in the attention, but at the same time realizing an embarrassment at being singled out of the crowd. It had been her habit for so long to blend in, to keep the boat from rocking, to avoid standing out and generating gossip, that even being sighted in a pretty dress was uncomfortable.

Well, she'd suffer through it tonight, she decided, her heart laughing deliriously. She couldn't remember being happier. She poked her chest out and walked a little taller, a whole millimeter taller. It was this vertical enhancement that enabled her to spot Gary as he stood talking to two gentlemen and a striking woman in a dress as black as her hair.

They appeared to be deep in discussion, and she hesitated, wondering if she should intrude or not. She still hadn't found Earl, and Justin was waiting for her. She could catch up with Gary later.

". . . a garbageman," she heard a woman's voice saying, somewhere to her right. It was like a television commercial for E.F. Hutton, when everything seemed to stand still and the only sound in the huge ballroom was the woman's voice. "He doesn't look like *my* garbageman," she said.

"Are you sure?" her friend asked. "Since when can garbagemen afford to attend charity balls?"

"Well, he's not *just* a garbageman. He owns a recycling center and has several other financial interests, but he told Stan that his primary concerns were in everyday garbage."

"You're kidding."

"No. Stan said he was fascinating to listen to. Depressing but interesting and very amusing. Stan liked him. He gave the man his card and wants to invest in some new project he's been talking about."

Rose had heard enough. Her anger swelled to explosion level. She was hurt and ashamed and mortified, too, but all she could feel at the moment was the outrage.

Without looking more than a foot in front of her feet, she approached him.

"Ah, there you are," he said, his familiar voice warm with pleasure. "I was beginning to think that I'd lost you for the rest of the evening. Rose, I'd like you to meet Councilman Yarrell and his wife, Judith. And State Representative Paul McManaway."

"How do you do. Hello," she said, shaking hands but unable to look them in the eye.

"I was just trying to convince Bob here to—"

"Excuse me. I'm sorry," she broke in, weak voiced, trembling with indignation. "But I'd like to leave now. Please."

With a quick glance she could see the concern on their faces and heard it in Gary's voice.

"What's wrong? Are you ill?"

"Yes."

"Has something happened?"

"No, no."

"Are you sure?" he asked, sensing the end of his world and not knowing why or what had happened. Fear sank in bone deep, and he felt half sick to his stomach.

"I'm so sorry," she said again to the most-official people she'd ever been close enough to spit on.

While the three of them murmured their understanding and sympathy to Rose, Gary was shaking hands and promising to get in touch with them soon. She didn't move until she felt his hand at her back, and then it was if he'd flipped her switch and she all but ran to the exit.

"Wait a second. Will you slow down?" He kept trying to take her arm, and she kept shaking it off. "Rose. Hold on. What's happened?"

She was slinking past people without seeing them and without touching them, like a black snake in a water maze. Her goal: to get out the end and disappear.

"Rose," he said, taking a tight grip on her arm to slow her down. "Is it Earl? Has something happened? Or Harley? Is he all right?"

She growled and tried to pull away to the anteroom a few short feet away, but he wasn't letting go.

"Talk to me," he said, his tone demanding as he turned her to him and locked his left hand around her right arm.

"No. Not here."

Clearly she wasn't ill, but furious—with him. He was so surprised, his hold slipped and she got away. He caught her again in the anteroom between an ancient bronze sacrificial wine holder from China, early Chon period, and a painted steel project by Robert Smithson —some other damn period.

"Yes. Right here, right now," he said. "I want to know what's happened. Why are you so angry?"

She stared at him for a moment, then glanced around to find only two other people in the room. She kept her voice low, but her emotions made it hiss.

"I can't believe you'd do this to me."

"What?"

"Buy those tickets and get me to come and make it seem like something special, and all you really wanted to do is meet rich people and get their backing for your stupid furnace."

"That's not true," he said, looking bewildered. "I did send the tickets, that's true. And I did want it to be special, but the rest—"

"I trusted you. I thought you knew how important this was to me. I worried about Harley and Earl, but it never once occurred to me that you would deliberately do something like this."

"What? What have I done?"

"Why?" she asked, forgetting to keep her voice down.

"Why what?" He was at the end of his wits and his voice rose as well, drawing unnoticed stares from the ballroom. "You're going to have to calm down and tell me what I've done. I don't know why I'm defending myself."

"You wouldn't. You have no pride. No, you have too much pride. That's what it is. But you should know by now that the world doesn't begin and end in garbage dumps."

His eyes narrowed for a moment as if he were trying to decode a secret message from an alien planet. Then, suddenly, awareness dawned in his expression. He released her and stepped away as if she'd turned slimy in his hands.

"Is that what all this is about?" he asked, overwhelmed with shock and a terrible squeezing ache in his chest. "What I do? The recycling center? The landfills? The incinerator? I wasn't supposed to talk to anyone about them tonight, was I? I wasn't supposed to tell anyone what I do for a living. If they asked, I was supposed to make something up. Lie. But I sure as hell wasn't supposed to tell anyone I was a garbageman, was I, Rose?"

"You could have told them you were something else, yes. It's not as if you hang off the back of a truck. You could have said—"

"Oh, but I do hang off the back of the trucks sometimes. Remember? I told you that the first day we met. You knew who you were getting involved with. I never lied to you. I told you I was a garbageman, and that's exactly what I am. And damned proud of it."

"You've made that very clear. Telling a state representative . . ."

"And you've made it very clear that you're ashamed of it." His words vibrated off the walls, sending back waves of hurt and disappointment. Anger too. "Well, I'll tell *you* something, Miss Rosemary Wickum. I don't have a thing in the world to be ashamed of. I don't have to go to fancy parties to pretend to be something I'm not, and I don't have to let pompous peaheads dictate what I do or build things I hate. I am who I am. I won't apologize or pretend otherwise. I'm not like you, Rose."

If she were still fighting mad, she might have asked what he meant by that last remark. But she wasn't angry anymore. She was thinking more clearly, and she knew what he meant.

"As for telling McManaway who I was and what I do, I didn't have to," he said, his voice cold and calm now. "I'm on his subcommittee for urban renewal and reform. Yarrell is working with the Planning Commission to get my incinerator approved. And in case you hadn't noticed, neither one of them was embarrassed to be seen talking to a garbageman tonight."

"Gary, I—" By the time she thought to beg his forgiveness for being shallow and stupid and selfish, he'd stepped around the last of the sculptures and disappeared.

She wasn't sure how long she stood there, wishing the last few minutes away, before the music seeped into her consciousness. The Patrons' Ball. She looked up. Too many accusing eyes stared back at her. She felt like Cinderella at 12:01. Her true identity exposed. Her dress tattered and torn. With no glass slippers to prove the miracle had ever happened. No Prince Charming to love her or come to her rescue. No fairy godmother to give her a second chance.

An incorrect analogy, really. She couldn't be Cinderella. Cinderella was good and sweet and kind. Rose was an ugly stepsister, hateful and mean, pretending to be Cinderella. Always pretending to be someone she wasn't.

Pretending not to care, when she did. Striving to look perfect, when she wasn't. Sacrificing her life to avoid gossip. Wasting a year and a half welding sculptures she hated to please other people. She was a great pretender, and not much more.

One would have hoped that seeing Harley and Earl in the gathering at the ballroom doors would be a relief. It wasn't. They walked toward her with mixed expressions of sadness, disappointment, regret, disapproval, and confusion. Harley tried to smile, he really did, but he couldn't quite manage it. He didn't understand, couldn't imagine why Rose would want to hurt Gary the way she had. He'd wanted Gary to stick around awhile.

Earl, on the other hand, looked resigned. He looked tired. Weary and reconciled to picking up the tiny pieces of her life once again. By the time he reached her, her gaze was locked firmly to the floor, where her hopes and dreams lay drained and desolate. She was prepared for his silent censure, assuming he'd simply take her arm and lead her away. The light touch of his fingers beneath her chin was a surprise then, and she looked at him.

"When you were young, you ran away from it. Then you came back and hid from it. And now you're trying to destroy it. You only get one chance, you know. So before you waste your only shot at this life, you'd better figure out what it is you're aimin' at," he said, then he slipped an arm about her shoulders, turned her, and led her away from the ball.

ELEVEN

The two-and-a-half-hour drive back to Redgrove the next day was difficult, to say the least. The strain between the passengers in the long black limousine was brittle and fragile. Gary's generous nature and the prepaid bills on the hotel suite and the limo contrasted like diamonds in a coal mine to Rose's egotistical, self-indulgent, and hypocritical behavior of the night before. No one spoke and they all found a window to stare out off, fearing that the slightest unguarded glance could disrupt the delicate balance of guilt, love, reproach, support, frustration, and crushing loss between them.

There had been a message waiting when they returned to their rooms, from Lu of all people, insisting that Rose make time to browse the Cannery—a building once owned by Del Monte, now converted into shops and restaurants—before she left San Francisco. Most important.

Not much of a shopper in the first place, Rose dismissed the suggestion immediately. Shopping and chocolate and long-distance running—or any of the other coping mechanisms other people used—had never worked for Rose. Alcohol was the traditional escape she was most familiar with, and she had been tempted.

She didn't sleep in the huge bed she'd planned to share with Gary that night. She'd cried some, but she couldn't sleep. She'd cried, not because he was angry with her, but because she'd hurt him. She'd cried, not because she was alone again, but because of the person she was alone with, the person she'd let herself become.

Who was she? When had she become so unthinking and cruel? Having felt looked down upon through most of her life, how could she belittle someone else? Having felt unloved, how could she forsake Gary's kindness and care for false preconceptions and narrow-minded intolerance? If she loved him—and the soul-crushing misery she was feeling actually confirmed that she did—how could she have treated him so badly? If she'd ever felt shame before, it was nothing to the self-loathing she felt now.

The old gas station seemed to be located at the farthest end of the world by the time they got home. Small. Shabby. Off the driven path. A nowhere place that she called home. She wandered restlessly through the garage, eyeing the near-finished but incomplete sculptures that stood in the shadows as the afternoon light began to fade in the windows.

Who was she? she wondered again. Small, shabby, frightened Rose. Living in a hole beside the ocean where no one would find her. Rigidly walking the lines down life's highway to avoid being noticed; to escape the pain of feeling too much; to evade other people's opinions and prejudices.

She was a void, she thought, running her hands across the cool, lifeless steel without feeling it. A good word, "void." She had depicted more of herself in these pieces than she realized. They were very much like her. She was a form that occupied space. She had very little spirit, no meaning. Even the motivation for their creation was bogus, and therefore they had no real purpose. If they had a function at all, it was for profit and recognition. Trifling ambitions. Very superficial. They were as empty as she was, just as insincere and just as contrived.

If true art is an extension of the artist's soul, she was one hell of a craftsman.

There was an almost-knock on the office door, a sort of on-the-way-through rapping on the glass as the door opened and Lu blew in.

"Rose?" she called, starting up the stairs, stopping midway when answered from below. "What are you doing here?"

"I live here."

"No, I mean, so soon. I just got back myself, and I wasn't at a ball last night. I had one, but I wasn't *at* one," she said, laughing at her own joke. "Tell me all about it. How was it? Give me every detail." She stopped. "What's wrong?"

"Me. Everything." As much as she needed someone to hold and comfort her, force of habit had her turning away to hide the extent of her pain. "Me, mostly."

"Why? What happened?"

"I don't know. Well, I do know, but I don't know how to explain it. . . . Actually, I can explain it, but I can't believe I did it."

"So, are you going to tell me what this thing that you know and can explain but don't believe is?"

Rose turned to face her, shaking her head, tears spilling onto her cheeks. "It's too awful. You won't want to know me anymore."

"Tell me anyway."

She lowered her gaze to the concrete floor. She walked slowly to the work table, seeing nothing. She picked up an old glove with a hole in the index finger and began to tell the story.

"And you haven't heard from him?" Lu asked when the tale was told and Rose was down to sniffing and wiping her eyes on her shirttail. "Well, it's only been a day. He's probably pretty mad still."

"I don't expect to ever hear from him again." Fresh tears pooled in her eyes. "Of all the people in the world to be mean and nasty to, why'd I have to pick on him?"

"Did you get my message about the Cannery?" she asked, offering no sympathy.

"Yes."

"I bet you didn't even go over and browse like I told you."

Rose scowled at her. "I was a little busy ruining my life at the time. I couldn't exactly take time out to go shopping, now could I?"

"I said browse. I didn't say anything about shopping.

There *is* a difference, you know. And now you'll just have to go back and do it."

"Some other time, all right?" she said, getting testy. For crying out loud. Shopping *and browsing* were the last things she wanted to do. She hated to shop, browsing was worse, and Lu knew it. Couldn't she see that Rose would rather be slitting her throat than *browsing?*

"Nope. Gotta go now," she said, ignoring the thorny inflection in Rose's voice. "You can use my car if you don't think your heap'll make it."

"Lu. I'm not going back to San Francisco tonight. Or any other time in the foreseeable future for that matter. I—"

"Yes you are."

"No. I am not." Now she was angry. "What is the matter with you? Can't you see I'm hurting here? My life—"

"*You're* hurting? *Your* life? See, that's the thing with people like us, Rose, it's always *our* pain. *Our* shame. *Our* life that's going down the tubes. We're so used to being hurt that after a while that's all we ever see. But think about it this time. Who hurt you this time?" She paused. "Gary? Or did you hurt yourself by hurting him?"

Her eyes narrowed in thought. "Yes. The second one. I hurt me by hurting him."

"So, technically, you're not really hurt. You just feel bad because you did something stupid. Right?"

"I guess." But miserable was miserable, wasn't it? No matter how you got there?

"Okay. Think it all the way through now. Are you

going to do what we usually do by locking yourself up with this imagined pain that's really just guilt for doing something you shouldn't have? Or are you going to do something about it? Are you going to close out the world again, spend your life alone or with a new man in your bed every night? Or are you going to break out of the pattern and go after the man you want?"

Rose wasn't missing the references Lu was making to her own life. She'd always suspected her past hadn't been pleasant, but she'd never thought to draw any comparisons between the two of them until now. In a way she supposed they were opposite ends of the same stick. Lu protected herself by dating one malleable young man after another until she was bored with them, never forming an attachment, and Rose survived by pushing everyone away from her to sustain her aloneness.

"Even if I wanted to break this . . . pattern you're talking about, what makes you think that Gary'll come back?"

"I don't think that. If I were Gary, I wouldn't have anything to do with you." She stopped to watch the hope drain from Rose's face. "But then again, I'm not Gary, am I? I can't say I'm sorry and I never learned to forgive—which is why I avoid situations where one or both might become necessary. I find it much easier to simply say good-bye."

Rose's heart went out to her, and to herself. Lu deserved a better life—and so did she.

How was it that Lu knew herself so well and yet hadn't tried to change? Was her pain so deep? Did she enjoy living alone with it? Rose looked at the rest of her life and found it long and bleak and lonely.

"I don't know what to do, Lu."

"Say you're sorry."

"That's it? Just—"

"No, no. Say it. Now. Out loud. Over and over. Practice it. Get used to saying it and to hearing it said out loud. It's not that easy. No one ever told us *they* were sorry, did they?" Rose glanced away and shook her head. "And we were always the ones getting hurt, so we've never had to say it, right? Well, you hurt yourself this time, and the only way you'll ever feel better about it is to make Gary feel better about it. You have to do whatever it takes to get him to forgive you. Now say it."

"What if he doesn't forgive me?"

"Then he doesn't. But you tried, and that's the first step to forgiving yourself. Say it."

"Lu?" she said, a nagging question filling her mouth so that to breathe, she had to spit it out. "If you knew this . . . about us . . . all along, why haven't you—?"

"Because I wasn't ready," she said, cutting her off, also slamming the door to any further questions. "But you are, so say it."

"I'm sorry."

"Again."

"I'm sorry."

"Keep going," she said, checking her tight jeans pockets for the right bulge before reaching in for her car keys. Meanwhile Rose chanted. "That's good. Now take my car and drive back down to the Cannery and—"

"But—"

"Yes, I know. You're sorry. You're sorry. Go on. I forgive you for doubting me. And I forgive you for not doing it this morning when I told you to," she said, putting the keys in the palm of her hand and pushing her toward the door. "See how easy it is?"

"But, Lu . . ."

"You don't even have to go into the stores. Window-shop."

"But, Lu . . ."

"No. I can't tell you," she said, turning Rose to the door every time she stopped and turned to protest. "You'll know it when you see it, and it'll clear up everything for you. It'll make saying you're sorry a little tougher in some ways, but in other ways it'll make it a whole lot easier."

"But, Lu . . ."

"I almost fainted when I saw it. You'll love it."

"Lulu!"

"What?"

She slapped the car keys back into her hand as she spoke firmly and finally.

"I have no idea what you're talking about, but if it'll shut you up, I'll go. First thing tomorrow."

"I can't wait that long."

"You're going to have to. They'll be closed by the time I get there."

"Oh. Right. I forgot. But first thing tomorrow . . ."

"Yes!"

"And then you find Gary and tell him you're . . ."

"Sorry," they said together.

The limo ride to San Francisco was a hard act for the old gray-green pickup truck to follow. The excitement of that journey was sadly eclipsed by the lamentable trip home, which made this third run along Highway 101 in less than forty-eight hours something of an exercise in self-control as Rose fought a constant urge to skip the side trip to the Cannery and head straight for the main event, apologizing to Gary.

The night had passed slowly as she accepted and rejected Lu's advice, over and over again. She knew asking Gary for forgiveness was certainly in order, and she wanted it more than anything. Except, maybe, for the ability to turn back time. She would have given anything to put everything back as it was, before she'd made that fateful trip across the ballroom.

But the possibility that her sin was too grievous to be forgiven and that she might have to face Gary's scorn and rejection had been enough to make her want to roll over, bury her head in the pillow, and forget the whole thing. She'd never claimed to be a brave woman.

By the time dawn crawled through her window, she was mentally adjusted. Despite all the nonsense with the Cannery, Lu was right about the importance of saying and hearing the words "I'm sorry." She'd dozed off and dreamt of her life as it might have been if her mother had had the chance and her father had thought just once to tell her they were sorry. She'd loved them. She would have forgiven them anything. . . . if they had asked.

She was grumbling mad by the time she entered the

Cannery. What had been a bleak overcast morning in Redgrove was now a rainy day in San Francisco. She'd found Columbus Street on the map easily enough, but finding it in the city traffic, and in the rain, was a whole other story. When she finally reached the foot of it and the Cannery was within sight, she couldn't find a parking place. She didn't know why she was there or what she was looking for, and she was wasting a lot of time when she should have and would have been looking for Gary.

A little over an hour later she was ready to choke Lu with her bare hands.

She'd scoured every window, one by one, restaurants included, looking for something, anything, just one single thing to jump out at her and scream, "I'm what you're looking for."

She meandered into a Chicken Delight and bought a lemonade to go. Whatever dress or pair of shoes or book or pen set or porcelain figurine or piece of jewelry Lu had insisted she come see, was now gone. Her feet were getting tired, and there was nothing in almost the entire shopping mall that had held her interest for more than a second or two.

She might have to come back, she decided, handing the cashier a dollar bill and waiting for the change. She was a rotten shopper to begin with, and she was so distracted by her eagerness to see Gary and get her apology over with that she probably wasn't browsing as well as she might under other circumstances. Lu would just have to understand.

Better yet, Lu could come back with her and show

her *exactly* what she wanted her to see, she thought, leaving the Chicken Delight. She'd wasted an entire morning on this hide-and-seek game and she was sick of it.

A kaleidoscope of sparkling multicolored lights from across the way caught in the corner of her eye. Instinctively she glanced at it, started to walk away, then glanced back. Her eyes narrowed for clearer vision. Her brows came together in confusion. Holding the lemonade in one hand and the straw in the other, she approached the twinkling lights slowly, as if they were reeling her in like a fish.

There in a darkened display window, set on a small turntable, under a hidden high-intensity light, was her sculpture. Steel and stained glass designed and welded as uniquely as if she'd given birth to it. She could remember making every inlay, bending each metal rod, brazing every raw edge, sanding, buffing . . . and giving it away to Gary.

There were emotions, both good and bad, stirring inside her, but she couldn't pick one to feel, and she didn't know what to think. She had questions, too, lots of them, the biggest being, what was it doing there?

She stepped back from the window, glancing about for the name of the store.

GARY'S GOURMET GARBAGE.

Well, that answered about half her questions right there. Who else? Was there any other man in the world whose name lent itself so well to the nation's waste—and now it's recycled—by-products?

The window on the other side of the entrance was

artfully crowded with recycled paper products: cups, plates, napkins, bowls, stationery, books, computer paper; gift bags, paper towels, storage boxes. A colorful cardboard mobile of ducklings and chicks hung from the ceiling.

She wandered inside. There were toys, clothes, quilts, chairs, and lamps, all new and all made of recycled materials. There were small displays for building materials such as insulation, plywood, abrasive paper made of glass for sanding, nails, oils, and cleaners. More displays for playground equipment, fertilizers, a walnut shell concoction for cleaning the bottom of boats and a . . .

"If you can't find it here, we can find it for you," a pleasant young female voice said behind her. "Are you looking for anything in particular?"

"No. Ah, I'm just browsing. Thank you."

"That's fine. Help yourself," she said, moving away to help another customer, of which there were surprisingly many. "We have another room in the back with some pottery and glass you won't want to miss. And we have catalogs at the front desk if you'd like to look at them or take one home. They're free. And someone up there can put you on our mailing list if you like."

"Thank you," she said, stunned. "Oh. You know, there is something you could help me with . . ."

"Yes?"

"That, ah, sculpture in the front window? How . . . how much are you asking for it?"

The young woman smiled. "I'm sorry, but it isn't for sale. It belongs to the owner and he won't sell it.

He's already had several people offer him money for it. But what he *will* do is take your name and address if you're interested, and when the artist is ready to sell others similar to it, he'd be very willing to send you the information. If you'd like to sign—"

"No. No. That's all right. I was just curious."

"Lots of people are. It's beautiful, isn't it?"

Rose nodded.

"Is there anything else you'd like to see?"

"No thanks, er, yes, actually. I'd like to see the owner. Is he here today?"

She grinned. "No, he isn't. He's not a very hands-on owner. I'm the manager. He just sort of pops in once in a while to check on things. But if you're thinking of making him a bid on the sculpture, I can tell you there's no use trying. He's very attached to it."

"Oh, no. Not the sculpture, I . . . I wanted to tell him how wonderful this store is. I never imagined . . ."

"It's pretty amazing, isn't it?" she said, glancing around the store. "People can be real inventive when they put their minds to it. And like I said, if we don't have it here, we can find it for you. My boss knows everything there is to know about recycling."

"Yes, he does. I mean, I can see that he does."

She could see many things she hadn't seen before. The extent to which he'd dedicated his life to cleaning up the earth and its atmosphere. The extent of his belief in the ingenuity of mankind. The extent of his faith in her talent. The extent of his love for her.

TWELVE

Centering in on Gary's general location might have been difficult for a common civilian outside the garbage loop.

Rose, however, knew from a couple of months of seeing him with a telephone stuck to his ear that his office *always* knew how to find him. And there was only one All Bright Garbage and Refuse Collection listed in the phone book. Unfortunately, it was an 800 number and they were disinclined to give out his exact whereabouts, even though they would gladly take a message.

Well.

Who did they think they were dealing with? Certainly not Rosemary Wickum, Junker Extraordinaire, Pooh-bah of the Royal Order of Rummagers, soon to be the next Queen of Trash. If she had her way. And she was praying she would, just this once. In all her life, just this once, she was going to have it her way. *She* had an ace in the hole.

"Cletus? Hello?" she said, picking up a pay phone when it rang. She'd been waiting and glaring off potential users for the past twenty minutes.

"Hey, Rosie," he said, sounding a million miles away. "I did what you said. I called the main office and told them I had to talk to the boss in person, but they weren't much help." *Now* she was starting to worry. "They said he'd be out all day. I guess he's someplace in Vallejo ridin' the trucks."

"You mean he's collecting trash? On the trucks?"

"Yeah. He does that sometimes. Says it keeps him humble."

"Yes, I know." She frowned and chewed her lower lip as she contemplated her choices. "Where *is* Vallejo, Cletus? Do you know?"

"North of you. On the other side of the Bay, I think."

"Which bridge would I take?"

"Hang on," he said, leaving the phone with a clatter and a clunk.

Rose fidgeted nervously waiting for him. Even if she could find Vallejo, what would she do then? Drive up and down every street looking for garbage trucks? That could take a week. No, not if she drove only the streets that had trash set out for collection.

And those would be?

Cletus returned to the phone with a map from his truck and she got directions to Vallejo, which she could have gotten from her own map, had she thought of it. She used a quarter to dial information and applied the charges to her home phone to call Vallejo's Sanitation Department. A phone card would have come in handy.

And what part of Vallejo had the trash picked up on Mondays? she asked the clerk in the Sanitation office. The northeast side, of course. North of Bella Vista, east of San Jacinto.

See? Almost simple.

Midday traffic was awful, and it was still raining intermittently. It took her almost an hour to get to Vallejo.

The corner of Bella Vista and San Jacinto was a busy intersection. She chugged the gray-green bucket of bolts and rust east two blocks and north three more blocks to a residential area.

She was in luck. It was a neighborhood with children. And no one takes notice of garbage trucks the way children do.

But because of the drizzly day, there weren't many kids out. Feeling a bit crazed by now, and far beyond caring what people thought of her, Rose found a yard with lots of bikes and balls in it and walked up to the door. A little boy about six or seven years old came to the door with his mother. He knew that the garbage truck had already passed by and it was going thataway—north.

Again she felt someone good was watching over her. Vallejo was one of those towns that divided its blocks with alleys, which meant she had only to search one alley for every two streets going north and south.

See? Almost simple.

She was really supersleuthing when she discovered

she could drive in and out of the alleys along one street going west to east to see if the trash cans were empty—that would mean that Gary had already been down that alley, of course. In fact, she was so busy and pleased with her sleuthing, she nearly forgot that with all the time she was subtracting from her search, she was also getting closer and closer to her moment of reckoning.

She understood that when she found her first full trash can, recycling bins beside it, heaped with cans, plastic milk jugs, and newspapers. Her palms grew moist with apprehension as she drove around the block to the last alley with empty cans and started north, across the next street and through the next alley.

What if he shouted at her? She hated it when people shouted at her. What if he refused to listen to her? Told her to go to hell? Wouldn't let her apologize?

She was tired, frightened, and guilty, and the rain was depressing. There didn't seem to be any end to it. A big black cloud would roll in from the sea, dump its load, and float off toward the mountains. Followed by another and then another. Taking any mental sidetrack she could, she wondered if anyone had ever identified the idiot who went around telling people that it never rained in California.

She wasn't sure if the sky was darkening with another storm front or if she was simply imagining the doom and gloom around her when she finally spied the sanitation truck in the next alley.

She slowed to a crawl—the old truck's favorite speed—and absently rubbed at the tight ache in her chest. Why hadn't she prepared anything? What was she going to say? Her mouth went dry and her throat closed up when a familiar form in blue overalls stepped off the back of the truck, walked with a long, lazy gait into the shadow of a small outbuilding, then reappeared with a trash can in each hand.

Gary wasn't sure if it was the incongruous and disturbing noises of a military all-terrain vehicle approaching or the eerie sense of being watched that caused him to look up. But seeing Rose's gray-green hunk-o-junk creeping toward him left him with the impression that it was probably both. It belched a rude cloud of black smoke as it stopped at the street. But it wasn't until it started to cross the street into the alley behind him that he chose to disregard the urge to meet it halfway and took up the impulse to ignore it.

Of course, it was an impetuous inclination that wreaked havoc on his nerves. Two minutes after leaving Rose at the Essex Hotel, he'd stormed out onto the sidewalk and felt besieged by the sounds and sights of the city—the tall buildings, the tiny lights in the dark, the rush of traffic, the hum of neon signs, the faces of countless strangers; rainwater gurgling in the gutter, sirens. The fog was so thin, it hardly impaired his vision, but instead distorted what he saw so that everything took on an unreal, unfriendly, unconnected, sort of a forsaken quality that made him want to cry out in loneliness.

He was smarting and he was angry, but with a sudden and horrendous jolt in the pit of his stomach, he felt something much worse. Lost and alone. He'd turned back to the hotel with every intention of returning to

Rose and doing whatever it took to work things out with her. But his pride stood stony and uncompromising between him and the door.

He'd taken his share of grief for a job and a cause he believed in. He could even understand Rose's frustrations in dealing with standardized pigeonholes and stereotypes, but he'd expected more from her than shame and embarrassment. Maybe he'd expected too much.

He'd asked the doorman to call him a cab and spent the entire ride—the entire and very expensive ride—back to his house in Fairfield wondering if he'd overreacted. People liked to think they were evolving, becoming more tolerant, more sensitive to the needs of others. But it was a slow and difficult process. There were still slanted suppositions toward alcoholism and judgments made on unwed mothers and prejudices against fatherless children. Maybe the struggle against all three was enough for one person's life. Maybe it hadn't been fair to ask her to put up with one more contorted opinion about her life.

He'd spent Sunday alone, rattling around in his semiempty house, seeing Rose everywhere. He picked up the phone a dozen times to call her, eager to forgive, then settled it back in its cradle, calling himself every kind of fool. She hadn't yet asked for forgiveness. She might not want any.

In the afternoon he tried to get some paperwork done and found himself making a list of alternative careers. Teacher. TV weatherman. Stand-up comedian. Truth was, he didn't want to be anything but a garbageman.

That's when he got mad again.

It wasn't in him to pretend to be something he wasn't. Isn't that what he'd told her? And wasn't it true? He was never going to be anything but an ordinary man who dealt with public waste on a day-to-day basis. It was a good, honest, and for him a lucrative profession. It didn't matter how much he loved her. If she couldn't accept who and what he was, she didn't really love him.

Yet, she was there. She'd come looking for him. He took it as a good sign, and his heart swelled with hope. But he cautioned himself to slow down. His whole world was at stake, and he needed to be sure. Sure that Rose could love him as he was. Even more sure that what he was wouldn't impair or betray Rose's faith in him.

He climbed back to his perch between the rear loader and the trailer of recycling bins and faced forward as they rolled to the next stop. He was traveling with the driver and the two regular loaders, who were keenly aware of the beat-up pickup truck following them, assuming it wanted to pass. He was the only man not surprised when a red-haired woman jumped out and left the poor old thing sputtering to death.

"Gary?" she said, walking around to the right side of the truck where he was tossing a heavy trash can up in the air to empty it into the truck as if it were a glass of water. She watched him pick up a second can and repeat the action, assuming he would turn to her when he was finished. He turned in the opposite direction as if he hadn't heard her speak and couldn't see her standing there. "Gary. Could we talk for a minute? Please?"

"What about?" He found he couldn't ignore her. Had he forgotten how beautiful she was? The humidity had frizzed her great mane of copper and gold curls, making them look soft and out of control.

"About Saturday night. At the ball. About what I did."

"What did you do?" He'd picked up two recycling containers and was sorting them into the appropriate bins on the trailer. Naturally, the two regulars, who were loading from the other side, were finished and terribly interested in the garbage groupie they'd picked up.

Rose glanced over the top of the trailer at the two loaders and then back to Gary, who was clearly disinclined to step away to have a private discussion with her.

"Well, I . . ." It wasn't ever going to be easy, she decided, jumping in with both feet. "I was thoughtless and rude and mean and nasty and—"

"When?"

She looked again at the men climbing onto the truck from the other side. When she looked back, Gary was again stationed on the right rear bumper. With a hiss and a squeal from the brakes, and the clank of loose glass and the tink of aluminum cans, the truck rumbled on to the next stop.

She raced back to her gray-patched monster. Twice she tried to get it to roll over. The third time it didn't mutter a sound. It was exhausted and sound asleep.

Meanwhile Gary's garbage truck had made two more stops. She had to jog-walk to catch up. When she did, she couldn't remember the question.

"I asked when it was that you were thoughtless and

mean and rude and nasty. My memory is a bit selective today."

About as selective as a hog in slop, she suspected. Still, it was his apology. He could take it any way he wanted to, so long as he took it.

"When I asked you not to tell people you were a garbageman." She waited for a response while he dumped two more cans. Nothing. He went back for the recycling. "It was a stupid thing to do. I knew it the second I did it. I know it hurt you, and I know you're angry."

"Excuse me," he said, indicating she was standing in his way. She stepped aside.

"I don't blame you," she said, leaning forward, trying to see his face. "I mean, I don't blame you for being hurt and angry. I would be too. There is no excuse for what I did, but I do have an explanation. If you want to hear it."

He was climbing back on the truck and it was starting to roll away when he looked down at her and said, "I'm listening."

She hustled along to keep up.

"Well, like I said, I have no excuse, but I did think it was important to impress those people that night. I'm ashamed to say it, but it's true. And you were right about me pretending to be someone I wasn't. At least you're honest. With the people you meet. And with yourself." He was already dumping newspapers. She'd have to talk faster, or she'd be miles away from her truck by the time he told her to get lost. "I used to be that way. Honest. I knew who I was and what I was and where . . . I came . . . from.

Next stop.

"I . . . I've always been affected by what I thought other people were thinking," she said, rushing on, a bit winded. "I hated it when people pitied me after my mother died. I hated that the whole town knew my dad was a drunk. I hated getting hand-me-down dresses because he couldn't hold a job and everyone knew we were living off Earl's pension. I hated going to school with bruises because everyone knew how I got them. I hated coming home a failure that first time I ran away because everyone knew I couldn't make it on my own. I hated coming home pregnant the second time because then they knew I wasn't any better than he was."

The truck was pulling away again. Gary, though he wasn't saying a word, was watching her with a grave expression. He still cared. He was listening.

He was also going around the block to the next alley.

Unpredictably, the tailgate of the trailer seemed to catch in her hands and she glommed on, leaping to secure the fender under her feet, her own tailgate jutting out over the road.

When they pulled out into the street, she looked around to determine the amount of traffic happening by to see her spectacular spectacle. . . . And there she was again, worrying what people would think of her. Strangers, in fact.

She didn't care.

Truthfully, it was fun, riding on the back of the trash

truck. They weren't going very fast, because it was a residential area and they were about to turn again. So it wasn't frightening at all. Of course, if she ever caught Harley doing it, she'd break both his legs for him. But . . .

She jumped off the trailer, smiling, when it came to a complete stop. For half an instant she thought she saw a spark of amusement in Gary's eyes. But it sure wasn't there when he came back to the truck with the cans.

"Where was I? Oh, yeah. Harley," she said, following him this time because she noticed three recycling bins at this stop—sometimes there was only one or two. When he picked up the glass and newspapers, she bent and snatched up the aluminum cans. "I hated raising Harley in a town where everyone knew about him. I didn't want to have to put him through all that. But it was a hell we knew, you know? I thought it could be a lot worse somewhere else. And I wouldn't have my dad or Earl around for whatever help they were. So I stayed. And I hated it. But I never had to pretend to be anything I wasn't. I'm not sure when all that changed."

Next stop. She power-walked it.

"I think it was a progressive thing," she said, approaching the recycling bins thoughtfully. "Like walking that tightrope all those years. I never dated. I never yelled at Harley when the windows were open. I didn't drink or smoke or swear. I avoided people so I wouldn't have to make small talk about my life. I was eighteen, nineteen, twenty, thirty years old. I was young and I wanted to play and dance and date and have . . . well, all the things other women have but . . . I was just too afraid and too tired of giving everyone something to talk about. I was sick of living in a fishbowl. I thought if I made myself as dull as dirt, pretended to be someone I wasn't, and watched my p's and q's, they'd forget about me."

From someplace woefully nearby, thunder rumbled and the sky grew darker by the second. Rose looked up to estimate the time of the next deluge and saw that Gary was looking skyward as well. When his gaze lowered, it met hers instantly. Holding on with one gloved hand, he stooped low on his spot and extended his other hand to her. She took it, and he towed her off the ground until she could reach the rider's platform with her feet.

It was a short ride to the next stop. Way too short. Standing close to each other, being careful not to touch each other yet intensely aware of the intimate size and shape of the other's body, of the heat and the smell and the taste of it, was exquisitely nerve-racking. The truck stopped, and he stepped backward off the platform and jumped down. Then he reached up for her.

Touching was a mistake. Even through his heavy canvas gloves and her jeans and jacket, they made contact. Deep in their souls. She came willingly, trusting him, and he caught her, sure and safe.

He hesitated briefly before he released her, then paused before he said, "Look. You don't have to say any more. I know how it was for you. And . . . I asked for it. I thought you and I had something special, and that if you didn't already think so, too, you would, in time. I was a fool."

"No," she said, sensing a change in him. Capitulation.

Lightning split the sky above them.

"I went romping into your life with my heart on my sleeve. I was reckless. I was so in love that I wouldn't listen when you told me you didn't want a relationship. I was a blind, drooling idiot who couldn't see that I wasn't the best you could do. I—"

"No. Stop," she said, grabbing the front of his overalls. Several big fat raindrops fell on her face. "You're wrong. Don't you see? You *are* the best thing that's ever happened to me."

"Not if you're embarrassed to be seen with me," he said, gently removing her hands from his chest and reaching for the big trash cans.

"I'm not," she said, watching him for a second, then hurrying over to fetch the trash set aside for recycling, which in her frenzied mind had become 'her job.' "Don't you see? You don't embarrass me, you scare me. Every time I'd try to run and hide from you, to protect myself from you, you'd find me and make me laugh. You made me happy and I started to like it. I started to care, and I was afraid of being hurt again. I've loved people before, you know. They hurt me and ignored me and left me all alone. I made up my mind years ago that I wouldn't need anyone in that way again. I wasted most my life thinking that."

The truck was ready to pull away again. She caught the driver's eye in the rider's side rearview mirror and used the hand signal she'd seen the men use to motion him on. She jogged ahead as the blackened sky opened and dumped its load.

The trash at the next stop wasn't in cans but tied up in large green plastic bags. She grabbed them both before Gary was off the truck, lugged them over to the loader, and threw them in. She was exceptionally strong for a girl.

Gary was practically standing still at the recycling bins when she spoke again.

"I know it's too late to change what I've done," she said, standing beside him, craning her neck to see his face. "And I know I don't deserve it, but I want a second chance."

She could have a million chances if she wanted them. He studied her over the blue and white bin and wondered at the cost of her being there. She was probably terrified, he thought, seeing only the sorrow in her eyes.

"I don't care what you do for a living," she said, raising her voice a little in the storm, and because his silence was peeling her nerves raw. The rain beat down on her head and dripped into her eyes. "I don't. All I care about is you. You could be a ditchdigger . . . No." There was probably some sweet, kind, loving, and truly terrific ditchdigger around somewhere too. "You could be a serial killer, and I'd probably still love you. I was scared. I was afraid of loving you too much, afraid you'd leave me. So I hurt you first. I didn't mean to. I didn't plan it. But I think all along some part of me was waiting . . . waiting for you to give me anything I could use to push you away."

He wanted to kiss her. He wanted to hold her in his arms and smooth the rain from her face. He wanted to stroke her stringy wet hair and tell her she was forgiven.

But first he was going to have to catch her.

She'd taken over the operation. She motioned the driver forward, walking alongside the truck, and left him holding two empty recycling bins. He tossed them in the correct general direction and started after her.

As it happened, the next house had only one trash bag and no recycling set out. She grinned at the regulars as they finished their side, *after her*, suddenly realizing that she didn't know who they were.

"I'm Rosemary Wickum," she said, and smiled at Felix and Germain as they introduced themselves. She hurried forward to hang on the door and meet the driver. Gary had only a couple of seconds to shake off his bewilderment before the truck started to roll again.

They were back to cans and bins at the next place. Rose chose the can, despite it's extra weight, because she found she preferred dumping to sorting.

Curious to see how far she'd go, Gary tended the bins and watched surreptitiously as she dragged the heavy can to the truck, grunting and groaning. Twice during her struggle to get the can into the air, he was tempted to help her. But he didn't. She was like a pressure cooker letting off steam. She was giving him time to think and consider his feelings toward her, getting down and dirty and burning off anxious energy while she awaited his decision.

He was vastly amused. And more in love with her than he ever imagined he might be. She was an odd woman, his Rose. When she appeared to be an impregnable fortress, she was most vulnerable. She thought loving was a weakness, and yet it was what she craved the most. She could bear the weight of shame for other people's actions, but her own mistakes were unbearable and unforgivable. She was bright and imaginative, and yet the simplest thing in the world, accepting love, seemed beyond her.

He endured the next two sets of cans because she seemed so determined to prove something to him. She kept looking his way, but didn't speak, and wasn't looking to be spoken to. It was almost as if she were challenging him in some way, as if she were trying to make a point.

Finally, when she was soaked with rain and her teeth were chattering from the chill, she staggered under the weight and lost her grip on the can. It made a terrible sound above the noise of the truck and the rain as it crashed to the ground. Her cry of defeat twisted his heart.

"Dammit, Rose, you don't need to be doing this," he said, angry that he hadn't stopped her earlier. "Are you all right? Did you hurt yourself? Your back?"

She'd bent down to pick up the mess of loose trash, and he went down to help her, trying to push her away at the same time.

"Stop it now," he said. "You're soaking wet and cold. Go sit up front with Harry."

"No." She was picking the trash up with her bare hands.

"Don't touch this, any of it. You don't know what's in it. Needles. Razors. Get back now. I'll do it."

"No."

"Dammit, Rose!" He stood up straight and tall to show her how big and strong he was, to let her know that if he had to, he'd use brute force to get her out of the garbage. "Get out of it."

"No," she said, standing up to show him she was only average height, to let him know that if she had to, she'd use her feminine limbs to pulverize his family jewels. "I want to help. I need to do this."

"It isn't necessary."

"It is necessary. It's important that I do this." He could see it was.

"Why? You don't have to haul garbage to prove you love me."

Watching from the other side of the trailer, Felix and Germain sighed with relief. They missed the good ol' days when garbage was garbage and they were garbagemen. Now it was all trash and recycling materials and sanitation workers. They had been very worried that Rose might be another new trend. A garbagewoman wannabe.

"I know that," they heard her say. She was looking like an indignant, half-drowned cat. "I don't have to prove anything to you, or anyone else. Certainly not my love. I wouldn't even be here if I didn't love you."

"I know," he said, standing perfectly still as he realized all his hurt and anger were gone, and that she'd just said she loved him, out loud, for the first time.

"All right then," she said, and, seeing that he no

longer cared to fight with her, she went back to cleaning up the spilled trash.

"Rose. Honey," he said, taking her hands in his. "Please don't do this. There are shovels if you're going to insist on it, but I really wish you'd stop."

"Please," she said, looking up at him, her eyelashes wet with rain—no, with tears. "Let me do it."

"Why? Why is it so important that *you* do it?"

"Because . . ." She made a vague gesture with her hands, which were still wrapped in his, and looked at him as if he should understand the significance, as if it were some common custom he should know about. When it was clear that he didn't, she was forced to explain. ". . . it's the only way I know to say I'm sorry."

His smile was slow and sweet, and the chuckle that rose in his chest was light and happy. He scooped her into his arms and held her close as the rain washed away the residue of her fear, his qualms, their queries into the future.

In that moment they knew the truth. They were going to build a life together. And in that life they were going to fight again and hurt again; they were going to face sorrow together and worry together and be disappointed together. Together they would love and laugh and cry; they would deal with the world and overcome any obstacle put in their paths. You see, they were in love, and for very different reasons they knew what a precious, fragile thing it was; that it needed to be cherished and nurtured and cared for . . . and never taken for granted.

"I love you," he said, his exultant words muffled in her hair.

"I know."

He laughed at her airy confidence.

"You think you're so smart." He whacked her wet backside, then fondled it. As long as his hand was there . . . "Two minutes ago you weren't so sure I was ever going to forgive you."

"Of course I was." She pulled away to look at him. "I wasn't sure you'd listen to my apology, but I knew you'd forgive."

"You did, huh?" He kissed her. "And what made you so sure?"

"Gary," she said, as if preparing to speak to a two-year-old. "I've been to the Cannery."

It was a second or two before the dawning comprehension cleared the darkness of confusion from his eyes. Then he looked sheepish.

"Were you mad? I know I should have told you about it, but . . ."

"But what?"

"Well, I didn't think you'd appreciate my interference."

"You were right, I wouldn't have."

"But you don't mind it now?" he asked, noting her lack of temper.

"I didn't say that, did I? What you did was . . . was sneaky and deceitful and wrong. You ganged up with Harley against me to make a point. You took it upon yourself to teach me a lesson in being true to myself. You thought you needed to show me that what I made from love was far more unique and beautiful and vital than what I made for money. You were arrogant and presumptuous to interfere."

"I know," he said, looking as guilty as Harley ever had, caught fair and square. "And I'm—"

"What I said was," she broke in to continue, "I wasn't sure you'd listen to my apology, because what I did was horrible. But the whole time I was looking for you, I knew that you'd forgive me, eventually, because I knew you loved me." He tried to say something, but she stopped him with her fingers to his lips. "What you did was probably wrong, but it was also necessary and good for me. You believed in me. You believed in what I do when I act from my heart. You did something no one has ever done for me before. What you did, I couldn't do for myself."

"So . . . you're not mad."

She shook her head and watched as his whole physique transformed before her eyes. From guilty and repentant to sure and cocky. Her sigh was both happy and reconciled.

"And you're beginning to see that what I told you about being a very bright guy wasn't a lot of hot air? Have we ever talked about my insight and wisdom?"

"Not today, we haven't. But then, you haven't told me you love me today either."

"I haven't?" He looked seriously worried. "Yes I did. Not two minutes ago. You said you knew it."

"You mumbled something, and, luckily, I knew what you meant. But I could hardly hear it," she said, stepping closer than close. Besides," she glanced down at her fingers as they fiddled with the collar of his overalls, then looked back, "I want to hear it again."

"You will," he promised, removing his gloves to push the wet hair from her face, to hold it gently between his palms. "I love you, Rose."

He lowered his lips to hers, as tender and engaging as his love for her.

Looking on, Felix and Germain clapped and whistled their approval. Harry honked the horn. They were glad everything had turned out well. And they'd be happier when the trash was finally cleaned up and they could be on their way. The boss wasn't a bad guy, but having him around always threw their timing off.

The King and Queen of Trash heard nothing but the pleasured moans from each other's throats. He deepened the kiss, and she pressed herself close to his heart. Their passion flowed freely; they were supercharged with excitement and desire. They were like two lightning rods standing in the rain, with garbage floating in a puddle of water at their feet and electricity cutting the air above them.

They never knew what hit them.

Even thirty years later.

THE EDITOR'S CORNER

Prepare to be swept off your feet by the four sizzling LOVESWEPT romances available next month. Never mind puppy love—you're soon to experience the tumultuous effects of desperation and passion in this spring's roller-coaster of romance.

Bestselling author Fayrene Preston turns up the heat with **LADY BEWARE**, LOVESWEPT #742. Kendall Merrick trusts Steven Gant when she should be running for her life. From the moment they meet, she is certain she knows him—knows his warmth, his scent, and the heat of his caress—but it just isn't possible! Steven hints she is in danger, then tempts her with fiery kisses that make her forget any fear. Has she surrendered to a stranger who will steal her soul? Find out in this spellbinding tale from Fayrene Preston.

Change gears with Marcia Evanick's playful but passionate **EMMA AND THE HANDSOME DEVIL**, LOVESWEPT #743. She figures Brent Haywood will be happy to sell his half of Amazing Grace, but when the gorgeous hunk says he is staying, Emma Carson wonders what he could possibly want with a chicken farm—or her! Fascinated by his spunky housemate, Brent senses her yearnings, guesses at the silk she wears beneath the denim, and hopes that his lips can silence her fear of never being enough for him. Discover if opposites really do attract as Marcia Evanick explores the humor and touching emotion of unexpected love.

THICK AS THIEVES, LOVESWEPT #744, is Janis Reams Hudson's latest steamy suspense. Undercover agent Harper Montgomery stands alone as his brother is buried, remembering how Mike had stolen his future and married the woman who should have been *his* wife. Now, ten years later, Annie is no longer the carefree woman he remembers. Harper is determined to learn the bitter truth behind the sadness and fear in her eyes—and find out whether there is anything left of the old Annie, the one who had sworn their love was forever. Janis Reams Hudson fans the flames of reawakened love in this sizzling contemporary romance.

Join us in welcoming new author Riley Morse as we feature her sparkling debut, **INTO THE STORM**, LOVESWEPT #745. If all is fair in love and war, Dr. Ryan Jericho declares the battle lines drawn! Summer Keaton's golden beauty is true temptation, but the software she has designed will cost him a halfway house for kids he counsels—unless he distracts her long enough to break the deal. Scorched by a gaze that lights a fire of longing, Summer struggles to survive his seduction strategy without losing her heart. Riley Morse creates a pair of tantalizing adversaries in this fabulous love story.

Happy reading,

With warmest wishes!

Beth de Guzman

Shauna Summers

Beth de Guzman	Shauna Summers
Senior Editor	Associate Editor

P.S. Don't miss the exciting women's fiction Bantam has coming in June: In **FAIREST OF THEM ALL,** Teresa Medeiros's blockbuster medieval romance, Sir Austyn of Gavenmore, in search of a plain bride, wins Holly de Chastel in a tournament, never suspecting her to be the fairest woman in all of England; Geralyn Dawson's enticing new charmer, **TEMPTING MORALITY,** has Zach Burnett conceiving a plan to use Morality Brown for his personal revenge—only to have the miracle of love save his soul. Look for a sneak peek at these dazzling books in next month's LOVESWEPT. And immediately following this page, look for a preview of the terrific romances from Bantam that are *available now!*

"Iris Johansen is one of the romance genre's finest treasures."
—*Romantic Times*

DARK RIDER

by the *New York Times* bestselling author

IRIS JOHANSEN

New York Times *bestselling author Iris Johansen is a "master among master storytellers"* and her bestselling novels have won every major romance award, including the coveted* Romantic Times *Lifetime Achievement Award. Now discover the spellbinding world of Iris Johansen in her most tantalizing novel yet.*

From the moment she heard of the arrival of the English ship, Cassandra Deville sensed danger. But she never expected the sensuous invader who stepped out of the shadows of the palms and onto the moonlit beach. Bold, passionate, electrifyingly masculine, Jared Danemount made it clear he had every intention of destroying her father. But he hardly knew what to make of the exquisite, pagan creature who offered herself to him, defiantly declaring that she

* Affaire de Coeur

would use his desire to her own advantage. Still, he could no more resist her challenge than he could ignore the temptation to risk everything for the heart of a woman sworn to betray him.

"Are you truly a virgin?"

She stiffened and then whirled to face the man strolling out of the thatch of palms. He spoke in the Polynesian language she had used with her friends, but there could be no doubt that he was not one of them. He was as tall but leaner and moved with a slow, casual grace, not with the springy exuberance of the islanders. He was dressed in elegant tight breeches and his coat fit sleekly over his broad shoulders. His snowy cravat was tied in a complicated fall and his dark hair bound back in a queue.

He is very beautiful and has the grace and lusty appetite of that stallion you love so much.

Her friend Lihua had said those words and she was right. He *was* beautiful. Exotic grace and strength exuded from every limb. High cheekbones and that well-formed, sensual mouth gave his face a fascinating quality that made it hard to tear her gaze away. A stray breeze ruffled his dark hair and a lock fell across his wide forehead.

Pagan.

The word came out of nowhere and she instantly dismissed it. Their housekeeper Clara used the term to describe the islanders and she would deem it totally unfit for civilized young noblemen. Yet there was something free and reckless flickering in the stranger's expression that she had never seen in any of the islanders.

Yes, he must be the Englishman; he was coming from the direction of King Kamehameha's village, she realized. He probably only wanted supplies or trade rights as the other English did. She did not have to worry about him.

"Well, are you?" he asked lazily as he continued to walk toward her.

He might not be a threat but she answered with instinctive wariness. "You should not eavesdrop on others' conversations. It's not honorable."

"I could hardly keep from hearing. You were shouting." His gaze wandered from her face to her bare breasts and down to her hips swathed in the cotton sarong. "And I found the subject matter so very intriguing. It was exceptionally . . . arousing. It's not every day a man is compared to a stallion."

His arrogance and confidence were annoying. "Lihua is easily pleased."

He looked startled, but then a slow smile lit his face. "And you are not, if you're still a virgin. What a challenge to a man. What is your name?"

"What is yours?"

"Jared."

"You have another name."

His brows lifted. "You're not being fair. You've not told me your name yet." He bowed. "But, if we must be formal, I'm Jared Barton Danemount."

"And you're a duke?"

"I have that honor . . . or dishonor. Depending upon my current state of dissipation. Does that impress you?"

"No, it's only another word for chief, and we have many chiefs here."

He laughed. "I'm crushed. Now that we've established my relative unimportance, may I ask your name?"

"Kanoa." It was not a lie. It was the Polynesian name she had been given, and meant more to her than her birth name.

"The free one," the Englishman translated. "But you're not free. Not if this person you called the ugly one keeps you from pleasure."

"That's none of your concern."

"On the contrary, I hope to make it very much my concern. I've had very good news tonight and I feel like celebrating. Will you celebrate with me, Kanoa?"

His smile shimmered in the darkness, coaxing, alluring. Nonsense. He was only a man; it was stupid to be so fascinated by this stranger. "Why should I? Your good news is nothing to me."

"Because it's a fine night and I'm a man and you're a woman. Isn't that enough?"

LOVE STORM
by Susan Johnson

"Susan Johnson is one of the best."
—*Romantic Times*

Desperate to avoid a loathsome match, Zena Turku ran from the glittering ballroom in the snowy night and threw herself at the mercy of a darkly handsome stranger. He was her only hope of escape, her one guarantee of safe passage to her ancestral home in the Caucasus mountains. But Prince Alexander Kuzan mistook the alluring redhead for a lady of the evening, the perfect plaything to relieve the boredom of his country journey. Only after her exquisite innocence was revealed did the most notorious rake of St. Petersburg realize that his delicious game of seduction had turned into a conquest of his heart.

Zena experienced a frightening feeling of vulnerability when this darkly handsome prince touched her; it was as though she no longer belonged to herself, as though he controlled her passion with his merest touch.

The prince must think her the most degraded wanton to allow him such liberties, to actually beg for release in his arms. A deep sense of humiliation swept over her as she tried to reconcile this astonishing, unprecedented sensuousness with the acceptable behavior required of young society debutantes. How could she have permitted these rapturous feelings of hers to overcome her genteel upbringing? Certainly the prince would never respect her now.

Zena's eyelashes fluttered up and she gazed surreptitiously from under their shield at the man who had so casually taken her virginity. He was disturbingly handsome: fine, aristocratic features; full, sensitive mouth; dark, long, wavy hair; smooth bronze skin. The brilliance of a huge emerald caught her eye as his hand rested possessively on her hip, making her acutely aware of the contrast between their circumstances. He was handsome, rich, charming, seductively expert, she ruefully noted. Plainly she had made a fool of herself, and her mortification was absolute. But then she reminded herself sharply that *anything* was superior to having to wed that odious toad of a general, and the prince *was* taking her away from St. Petersburg.

The emerald twinkled in the subdued light as Alex gently brushed the damp curls from Zena's cheek. "I'm sorry for hurting you, *ma petite*," he whispered softly. "I had no idea this was your first evening as a streetwalker. Had I known, I could have been more gentle."

At which point Prince Alexander was presented with some fascinating information, most of which he would have quite willingly remained in ignorance of.

"I'm not a streetwalker, my lord."

Alex's black brows snapped together in a sudden scowl. *Bloody hell, what have I got into?*

"I'm the daughter of Baron Turku from Astrakhan."

The scowl deepened noticeably.

"My father died six months ago, and my aunt began trying to marry me off to General Scobloff."

The frown lifted instantly, and Alex breathed a sigh of relief. At least, he mentally noted, there were no irate relatives to reckon with immediately. "Sweet Jesus! That old vulture must be close to seventy!" he exclaimed, horrified.

"Sixty-one, my lord, and he's managed to bury two wives already," Zena quietly murmured. "I didn't want to become his wife, but my aunt was insisting, so I simply had to get away. My little brother and I will—"

"Little brother?" Alex sputtered. "The young child isn't yours?" he asked in confusion, and then remembered. Of course he wasn't hers; Alex had just taken her virginity! A distinct feeling of apprehension and, on the whole, disagreeable sensations struck the young prince. *Merde!* This just wasn't his night! "You deliberately led me on," he accused uncharitably, choosing to ignore the fact that he had drunk so much in the past fifteen hours that his clarity of thought was not at peak performance.

"I did not lead you on!" Zena returned tartly, angry that the prince should think she had contrived this entire situation. "Modest young ladies of good breeding do not lead men on!" she snapped.

"Permit me to disagree, my pet, for I've known many modest young ladies of good breeding," Alex disputed coolly, "a number of whom have led me on to the same, ah, satisfactory conclusion we have just enjoyed. They're all quite willing once the tiresome conventional posturing has been observed."

The prince's obvious competence in an area of

connoisseurship completely foreign to Zena's limited sphere served to squelch her ingenuous assertion.

Alex sighed disgruntledly. *Good God, for which of my sins am I paying penance?* "What am I to do with you—a damnable virgin? Of all the rotten luck! You try to be helpful and come to the aid of what appears to be a nice, ordinary streetwalker and look what happens. She turns out to be a cursed green virgin with a baby brother to boot, not to mention a respectable family."

"No, my lord, no family," Zena quietly reminded him.

A faintly pleased glint of relief momentarily shone in the depths of the golden eyes. "Thank God for small favors. Nevertheless, you, my dear, have become a vexatious problem," Alex censoriously intoned.

"You could take the honorable course of action and marry me, my lord."

PROMISE ME MAGIC

by the extraordinarily talented

Patricia Camden

"A strong new voice in historical fiction . . . This is an author to watch!"
—*Romantic Times*

With a fury born of fear, Katharina had taken aim at the bandit who dared to trespass on her land and fired only to discover that the powerful warrior she felled was a man she thought long dead . . . a man who had stolen her fortune . . . a man she despised. Now, as she gazed into Alexandre von Löwe's smoldering gray eyes and felt the overpowering pull of his attraction, she wondered why she'd let the scoundrel live and how she was going to tell him she was masquerading as his wife. . . .

"I am Katharina von Melle," she told him, then waited as if expecting a response.

"Madame von Melle," he said, giving her a slight nod. He grimaced and bit back a ripe oath. Someone had just lit the powder touchhole of the cannon in his head.

"Katharina," the woman gritted out as if to a slow wit. "Anna. Magdalena. von Melle."

Obviously, she thought he should know her. A

memory niggled, but it was beyond grasping in his fuzzy head. Christ, she was beautiful. Full lips hinting at a sensual nature that belied the coldness in her eyes, the bones—if not her manner or her clothes—telling of well-bred nobility.

A former lover? Had he passed the long months of a year's winter quarters spending his passion in that glorious voluptuous body? One forgot a great many things in war, some by accident, others for the sake of sanity, but, sweet God, he'd take her gun and shoot himself if he could ever have forgotten that body—or those eyes.

Katharina von Melle. It felt as if he should remember it, but . . . nothing. "Madame von Melle, of course!" he prevaricated. "The wounds of war have addled my wits. Such eyes as those would be forever burned into any man's memor—" The slender finger curling on the trigger tightened. "I mean, that is—"

" 'I mean, that is' . . . utter nonsense, Colonel von Löwe," she said, her gaze as steady as a cat's. "If there is any burning to be done, it will be into your body by a lead ball."

As a cat's . . . Katharina von Melle. *Oh, Jesus.* "Kat," he said. "You're Father's Kat." They had never met, but he knew her. God save him, he knew her.

"You blanch quite nicely," she told him. "I take it you recognize the name? Your *ward,* my dear Colonel. I was your ward. First your father's, then *yours.* Do you remember now? I was part of your inheritance, remember? Your eldest brother was to get the north end of this valley, complete with the lucrative mill, your middle brother was to get all the land in the middle, from the peak known as the Mule in the west to the Carabas River. And you—all you were to inherit was the small manor house of Löwe and a mangy spinster named Kat. And you did inherit. First the house and me, and then the rest of it when your brothers died, and all without bothering to leave your precious war."

He wanted to sleep and the careless irritation that comes from being deprived of it was gnawing at his sense of preservation. "Did you truly expect me to leave my regiment and come home to a ramshackle old house to nursemaid the bastard daughter of some friend of my father's I don't even know? The French had entered the war! Old alliances were falling apart; new alliances were being formed. It was as if a puddle of mercury had dispersed into a hundred bubbles, some that would save you, others that would prove fatal." He shrugged, but had to look away from the winter in her eyes. "An ink-stained lawyer's clerk sent word that you were living with friends in the Tausend capital. It seemed adequate to me. I had more important things to deal with—such as a war."

"War or no, alliances or no—you still managed to turn inheriting this Kat into a profit, didn't you? A ten-thousand thaler profit! My marriage portion. But I didn't know that then, did I? No. I discovered it six years ago when word came that you were dead. At last! At age twenty-two I found myself mistress of my fortune and my fate—except, of course, that there was no fortune. That loss cost me dearly, von Löwe. But though you cost me while alive, by being dead you have managed to partially pay me back. Löwe Manor is mine."

"Impossible."

"No, Colonel von Löwe, *possible*. In fact, more than possible. It has been done. A fait accompli. Löwe Manor is mine. For four years I have lived there, and no one has challenged me." A mixture of guilt and bravado flashed through her eyes, the same look a woman gets who has cheated on her lover and now seeks to deny it. He had barely registered that it was there before it was gone. She sighted again down the barrel of the pistol with renewed determination.

"And now, Colonel, though you neglected to give me a choice about my future when you stole my fortune from me, I shall give you a choice about yours. You can choose to leave—with Löwe remaining in my possession—or you can choose to contest my ownership. Of course, if you choose the latter, the hero dies, shot for a brigand on his way home. Such a shame."

"So the bastard daughter would turn murderer? Such a shame."

He heard her lick her lips. "You and Tragen and the other one can move to Alte Veste. It is but a day's ride from here."

"A day's ride straight up. It's coming on to winter, Kat . . . Katharina," he said carefully. "Alte Veste is deserted, and has been for three generations. Cold, too, and full of drafts. Tragen would probably succumb."

He waited, his breathing nearly suspended. He needed the obscurity that Löwe Manor could provide—at least until late February or early March. And after that, given von Mecklen's delight in all things ravaged, they all would most likely be looking for a new place to live. If they were still alive.

"You may stay until Tragen has recovered enough to travel. But you must give me your word that Löwe is mine."

He sucked in a breath of victory. "You have it."

"Say the words."

"I give you my word that Löwe Manor will be yours."

"Not will be . . . *is!*" She moved around to where Alexandre could see her, and what he saw made him go still inside. Distrust, despair, and an iron will to go on. It was the look of a woman touched too closely by war. He'd seen it before, on other women's faces, on those who had survived.

"Löwe is yours," he said softly.

"And . . . and you must accept whatever you find there."

He narrowed his eyes. "Why? What will I find there?" She did not answer. "What will I find there, Kat?" Silence. He let his head fall back to the folded wool, but through his lashes he could still see the black point of the pistol barrel aimed at him. "I will accept whatever I find there . . . within the restrictions of my oaths to the emperor, the duke of Tausend, and my men."

The gun barrel did not waver for a heartbeat. Then two . . . three . . .

"Cross me and you're a dead man," Katharina said with the tempered steel of conviction. And lowered the pistol.

He closed his eyes in relief. Whatever desperate hold he'd had on his awareness left him then, and he began to slip into sleep.

A nudge roused him to semiawareness. "Colonel

von Löwe," she called, nudging him again. "Colonel, there's one thing you should know before we reach Löwe Manor."

He grunted, drifting back into oblivion.

"I'm your wife."

Alexandre woke up.

Official Rules  **No Purchase Necessary**

To enter the sweepstakes outlined below, you must respond by the date specified and follow all entry instructions published elsewhere in this offer.

Dream Come True Sweepstakes

Sweepstakes begins 9/1/94, ends 1/15/96. To qualify for the Early Bird Prize, entry must be received by the date specified elsewhere in this offer. Winners will be selected in random drawings on 2/29/96 by an independent judging organization whose decisions are final. Early Bird winner will be selected in a separate drawing from among all qualifying entries.

Odds of winning determined by total number of entries received. Distribution not to exceed 300 million.

Estimated maximum retail value of prizes: Grand (1) $25,000 (cash alternative $20,000); First (1) $2,000; Second (1) $750; Third (50) $75; Fourth (1,000) $50; Early Bird (1) $5,000. Total prize value: $86,500.

Automobile and travel trailer must be picked up at a local dealer; all other merchandise prizes will be shipped to winners. Awarding of any prize to a minor will require written permission of parent/guardian. If a trip prize is won by a minor, s/he must be accompanied by parent/legal guardian. Trip prizes subject to availability and must be completed within 12 months of date awarded. Blackout dates may apply. Early Bird trip is on a space available basis and does not include port charges, gratuities, optional shore excursions and onboard personal purchases. Prizes are not transferable or redeemable for cash except as specified. No substitution for prizes except as necessary due to unavailability. Travel trailer and/or automobile license and registration fees are winners' responsibility as are any other incidental expenses not specified herein.

Early Bird Prize may not be offered in some presentations of this sweepstakes. Grand through third prize winners will have the option of selecting any prize offered at level won. All prizes will be awarded. Drawing will be held at 204 Center Square Road, Bridgeport, NJ 08014. Winners need not be present. For winners list (available in June, 1996), send a self-addressed, stamped envelope by 1/15/96 to: Dream Come True Winners, P.O. Box 572, Gibbstown, NJ 08027.

The Following Applies to the Sweepstakes Above:

No purchase necessary. No photocopied or mechanically reproduced entries will be accepted. Not responsible for lost, late, misdirected, damaged, incomplete, illegible, or postage-die mail. Entries become the property of sponsors and will not be returned.

Winner(s) will be notified by mail. Winner(s) may be required to sign and return an affidavit of eligibility/release within 14 days of date on notification or an alternate may be selected. Except where prohibited by law, entry constitutes permission to use of winners' names, hometowns, and likenesses for publicity without additional compensation. Void where prohibited or restricted. All federal, state, provincial, and local laws and regulations apply.

All prize values are in U.S. currency. Presentation of prizes may vary; values at a given prize level will be approximately the same. All taxes are winners' responsibility.

Canadian residents, in order to win, must first correctly answer a time-limited skill testing question administered by mail. Any litigation regarding the conduct and awarding of a prize in this publicity contest by a resident of the province of Quebec may be submitted to the Regie des loteries et courses du Quebec.

Sweepstakes is open to legal residents of the U.S., Canada, and Europe (in those areas where made available) who have received this offer.

Sweepstakes in sponsored by Ventura Associates, 1211 Avenue of the Americas, New York, NY 10036 and presented by independent businesses. Employees of these, their advertising agencies and promotional companies involved in this promotion, and their immediate families, agents, successors, and assignees shall be ineligible to participate in the promotion and shall not be eligible for any prizes covered herein. SWP 3/95